Ysatis De Saint Simon

Jesus
Stories of His Infancy

True Stories You Never Heard Before

Ysatis De Saint Simon
Jesus
Stories of His Infancy

True Stories You Never Heard Before

Jesus
Stories of His Infancy

Photographs from the film of *'A Child Called Jesus'* a Taurus Film and Pandora Film production courtesy of Pandora Film, Cologne, Germany, additional art masterpieces include, but are not limited to, cover *'The Good Shepherd'* and *'The children of the Shell'* by Bartolome Esteban Murillo *'The Garden of Venus'* by Titian *'Jesus Amongst the Doctors'* and, *'The Shepherds and The Angels'* by Carl Bloch, *L'Amour au Repos'* and *'Cupid and Psyche'* by William A. Boguereau' courtesy of Fine Arts Images, Inc. My deepest gratitude to all for making this book all the more beautiful.

ISBN: 978-1-5850-0403-4 (sc)
ISBN: 978-1-4208-7700-7 (e)

Print information available on the last page.

1stBooks - rev. 08/05/05

Jesus
Stories of His Infancy

The Seventh Angel Productions

Introduction

The stories of the infancy of Jesus that you are about to read are told by Mary of Bethany, later known as Mary of Magdala and are some of the most pure, powerful and illuminating teachings of the Child Jesus. Her older sister Martha, her baby brother Lazarus and Mary herself were very close to Jesus and loved Him since they were children, they were witnesses to many of the miracles Jesus did when He was an infant and a young man. Here are some of the stories she told later to many that came to her to learn about Jesus, His life and His Love. . .

Jesus illumined my childhood with His Light and His Love, when He left the stories my father used to tell us abut Him helped me to know Him better and to have Him as my friend and it is my hope that they will do the same for you. These stories are true stories, although sometimes they may seem unbelievable because they are magical and full of wonder. But we must remember that Jesus was a Divine Child, not just a child, I know that well. These are some of the most beautiful stories of His childhood that I know. There are many others that I would have loved to tell you, but I am forced to stop writing if I want to finish this book and offer it to you. So to my chagrin, I could not include all of the wonderful stories that I know about Him.

In the back of the book you will find four prayers that I said to Jesus every night before I went to bed. And after I closed my eyes I always felt that His Love surrounded me and I could go to sleep and have no fear, even if it was dark. There are also some exercises that will help you go within your self and see the Inner Light that shines within all of us and gives us His Peace. The Light Inside helps us to face all things for It is warm and makes us feel Love. It is His Light, and Jesus wanted us to know It, for He said many times to us that *the Kingdom of Heaven is within us.*

If you want to be happy and have a good life, regardless of what is going on around you, practice the exercises with patience and everyday, then your Inner Light will get brighter and brighter and the music better and better, until one day all you see will be that wonderful Light that makes the heart happy and you will hear all the time that beautiful sound that calms the mind in just one stroke.

In the beginning
Was the Word
And the Word
Was God
And the Word
Was with God
And the Word
Incarnated
And walked amongst men

Infancy

'There are a great many other things
that Jesus did, which, if they were written
one by one, not even this world, I believe,
Could contain the books that would be written. . .'

Saint John 21. 25

They left in the middle of the night, 'How beautiful,' Mary said. 'It is as if all the stars of Heaven have come down from heaven to illuminate His way. . .'

How did it all start?   As long as I can remember I first heard about Jesus the night of our flight to Egypt. . .   My name is Mary, I was almost a year old. . .   My parents although they were Essenes, were married. Marriage was not forbidden among the Essenes, as it was commonly believed, but their ideals regarding marriage were very high, and only a certain number of them were permitted to marry. At the time of our flight Martha was three, and Lazarus was about to be born. . . Our family, as many others, had to flee Judea partly because of the injustices of King Herod and partly because some Essene families had been selected by the Brotherhood to go to Egypt and locate in certain places to serve the Holy Family in case that they needed assistance. My father explained to Martha that part of the service, telling her that it was a high privilege to have been chosen to serve God on this earth, for the Baby was God incarnated. But because some people were not happy about His coming we all had to go away and be extremely quiet and quick. He said that we were going to a far away land and that she ought to be a very good girl a good example for me. He stressed to her that she should remember at all times, that this was not entirely a pleasure trip. That it was a good thing to remember at all times, that we were running away and hiding from soldiers who had orders to stop us and kill all the children under a certain age, especially if they were Essenes as we were. And when Martha asked, *'Who would give orders to kill children? And why is he doing that?'*

Our father explained to her the truth. . . I can remember clearly his answer, as if this had happened only yesterday, *'Herod, the Tetrarch of Judea, my princess,'* He said, *'because he lives in fear of someone taking his crown away from him. And fear comes out of the ignorance of men. One day I will tell you the whole story. . . We don't have time now, but there is always time to tell the good side of the story, so, I will tell it as we get ready to go. On this earth all things always have a good and bad side to them. What is good in this story is immense Martha, bigger that the sky. . . For the birth of this Baby is the best and the greatest thing that has ever happened on earth!'*

And then he added, *'You children, have an ability to understand these things better than we grown-ups do. If there were only children on earth we would not have to run away because everyone would be celebrating the birth of Baby Jesus. But things are not that way. We, in the Essene Brotherhood have expected His birth for hundreds of years because, my princess, It is the Word of God who has been born in this Child! He is our Savior and our King and of all men of God, so the Essene colony is rejoicing because this Baby's birth brings salvation to earth!'*

'And why does the earth need salvation?' Martha asked. And my father replied, *'Because man have forgotten the Kingdom of Heaven where they came from, and they do not know who they are anymore. And the Baby is here to bring us back home. So we rejoice but not everyone feels the same way, because not everyone Understands.'*

And Martha replied, *'Like the bad king. And why is the bad king afraid of a Baby if he is a king? Aren't kings supposed to be all-powerful? You are not afraid of me when I get angry, you just talk me out of it. Why then, is he afraid of a Baby?'*

And my father answered her, *'Because King Herod is not afraid of the Baby's anger, what troubles him is that he thinks that the Baby will take from him the crown of Judea! However, Baby Jesus is a Heavenly King, when He was born the heavens opened and the angels sang that the King of kings, the Highest God had been born on earth and a prophecy that says that the King of the Children of Light was going to be born in Bethlehem was fulfilled with His birth. This should have let Herod know that the Baby is not here to take his crown, but fear and ignorance blind him and make him do evil things, he lives in constant fear that someone will take his place of power, he fears even his own sons, so he wants to kill the Baby to protect his crown and has given orders that all children under two years old be killed, this is why we must go because your little sister and the baby that is coming are in danger. Now we must be very quick,'* he said, *'we must hurry to leave our home and go to a far away land. We must be very quiet, run away fast and hide well, I will see to it that we all do it really well, for it is my duty to protect all of you. Promise to be a very quiet and a very good girl and help us to see that your baby sister is as quiet as you are.'*

It is strange; I was not even one year old, but that moment and everything my father explained is still clear in my mind, as clear and fresh as the sunrise I see every morning.

After a silence I remember Martha asked, *'And what is an Essene'?*

My father smiled and said, *'Just people who aim to maintain humbleness before God and manifest justice towards all men; to do no harm, either by their own will or at the command of others to any living creature and to practice Love.'*

And then she asked, *'And, are we friends of the Baby-God?'*

And he replied, *'Yes. We are more than friends to the Baby-God, we are His humble servants, and we are grateful and honored to be so. We have looked forward to the coming of the great Saviour, who would be born within the fold of our Brotherhood. And He is here now! It is the greatest thing that could have ever happened to us, to be alive and to be of service to Him and to His family Martha. Yes, we are His friends and He has blessed us with His Very Special Friendship. . .'*

I think that neither Martha, nor I ever forgot these words. . . And who knows maybe even Lazarus, who was in our mother's womb, may have retained them because we were all in love with Jesus, way before we even met Him. . . Later on, I remember Martha asked how old was the Baby-God and my father said the He was just a few days old, few months less that the age that I was! I remember how proud I felt when I heard that the Baby was closer to me in age than to Martha! Then Martha asked if the Baby-God had a name? And my father said that His name was Jesus and that name was given to His mother by an angel. . .'

Then Martha asked, *'An angel from heaven, like my guardian angel? Did my mother get Mary's name and my name also from an angel?'*

And my father said, *'No, not everyone gets an angel to give them their name, He is a divine being Martha, remember that no matter how similar he looks to us, He is not just human. That is why His name is hallowed, the sound of His name is charged with divine power, the power of Life, which is the basis of our breath and all life there is. . . His name Jesus is as good to pronounce for us as it is to breathe. Call Him by His name when you have fear, or feel sad and He will help you, His name is like a bridge between our need and Him, so it is good to remember it. Would you like to say it now?'* He asked her, and she closed her eyes and said, *'Baby Jesus, be my friend,'* and she smiled. When she opened her eyes she said that she had seen Him smiling at her.

And my father said to her, *'You may want to say this to Him every night, 'Little Baby-Jesus, light of my life, you are a small child, just as I am, this why I love you so much and I give you all my love and all my heart tonight!'*

Martha loved that and since that day she talked to Jesus like this every night before she went to sleep, and so did I. Jesus! I liked the sound of the name of the Baby-God and started to repeat it over and over again in my mind. And I remember than wonderful things happened when I did! Like, I would feel calm and I could even see the air as little sparks and waves of light dancing over my crib, and I could hear a sound as if of little bells and crickets put together that made my heart happy! Whenever I was afraid, and that was often, because I was afraid of the dark. . . I would ask Jesus, the Baby-God to come and sleep with me. . . And I could see Him come into my crib and I would fall asleep and fear no more. So, His name was good to me when I was a baby for what it did and also because It was easy and soft to pronounce. . . As children often do, Martha wanted to know more about the Baby and asked many questions, I was glad because I also wanted to know but I couldn't speak well yet.

'Is king Herod going to kill the Baby?' Martha asked.

And our father answered, *'No, King Herod won't be able to kill the Baby, he has no power over Him. His parents have already left. . . And Archangel Gabriel and a host of His angels protect their flight. The Baby will grow to be wise, and strong and handsome and be the perfect Man. Herod fears because fear is part of him and of his life. This Baby is not like you, my princess, or like any other baby, He is the Heavenly Messiah, a Mystery made flesh - no human being will be able to kill Him, death has not power over Him, for He is Life Itself. He may seem to be just a baby, but He is not, He's the Old of olds, He seems to have just been born, but He's the one who has given birth to all life! King Herod is afraid of His power because the prophecies say that this Baby has come to establish His kingdom on this earth, but he just does not understand that Jesus has no need of his crown, nor of any kingdom of this world, for He is the King of all Universes, the Creator, Sustainer and Master of all Life.*

The Time of times will come when the stars above the Great Pyramid of Egypt finish their cycles and revolutions and align themselves above it again, as they were placed when the earth was born. . . At this time, the earth will undergo big changes and be made new, so that it can enter into this new dimension that He has come to open for all of us. . . A new place, which we call His Kingdom. . . Where there is no need, no want, no death, for all is perfect. When the Time of Renewal comes, all those who belong in His Kingdom will be made new and enter this perfect place. . . The divine Baby Jesus has been born my princess, just to show us the way to that perfection. . . And to open up the doors of heaven for us. That's the only reason why He has been born.'

Ah! Grown ups think babies do not understand what they say! How wrong they are! The words of my father stayed in my heart like a bird imprisoned in a golden cage . . . The memory of other things from that early period of my babyhood is very faint, almost gone, as if someone has erased them from my mind; but the words of my father about the divine Baby, the stories about His wondrous birth, their flight to Egypt, the adventures they had in the desert and everything else He did and said during His stay in our home, have always stayed vivid and clear in my mind just as if they happened yesterday! Yes, Jesus was part of my childhood dreams and fantasies, whenever I would be lost in my dreams I searched for Him and He always rescued me and showered me with light and we played with stars and with angels. I felt as if my love for Baby Jesus had been stamped on my consciousness even before I was born. . . As if I had always known Him and always longed for Him.

My father talked often about Jesus, he would tell us many stories, some about Mary, His Mother and some about Jesus, but we all liked to hear over and over again how He had been born that Holy Night and all the things that the shepherds said. Jonathan, a man my father knew well and who had interviewed the shepherds that were there, said that the shepherds had told him of many wonders and prodigies, which happened that night. That they were watching their flocks at night in Shepherds' Field, near Bethlehem, and had made fires to warm themselves because the night was cold and chilly, and that some kept watch, while others were asleep, when suddenly they were awakened by those who kept watch who asked,

'What does all this mean? Look at the sky, how light it is! But it's only the third watch, so it can't be daylight. . . Look! Wake-up, wake-up! Look! There are angels streaming down from the very vaults of heaven!'

And that all who were present said that there was a midnight light more brilliant than the sun which illumined everything but didn't hurt their eyes and that there was a new star shining straight on top of a cave where there was an animal's manger. The shepherds said that it seemed to them that the heavens had moved and that the configurations of the stars had changed! It seemed to them as if all the angels of heaven had come down to earth and were singing glory and pouring their light on the cave which seemed to be the center of their celebration and that the air seemed to be filled with voices saying,

'Glory, glory, glory to the most High! Happy art you Bethlehem, for God has fulfilled His promise to the fathers; for in thy chambers is born the King that shall rule in righteousness.'

Their shoutings would rise up in the heavens! And then would sink down in mellow strains, and roll along at the foot of the mountains, and die away in the most soft and musical manner they had ever heard! Then it would begin again high up in the heavens, in the very vaults of the sky, and descend in sweet and melodious strains!

There was a new star shining straight on top of the place where He was born. . . The shepherds said that it seemed to them the heavens had moved and the configurations of the stars had changed.

So, that they could not refrain from shouting and weeping at the same time! They said that the light would seem to burst forth high up in the heavens, and then descend in softer rays and light up the hills and valleys, making everything more visible than the light of the sun, though it was not so brilliant, but clearer like the brightest moon!

Jonathan asked the shepherds if they were not afraid? They replied that at first they were; but after awhile the light seemed to calm their spirits and so filled their hearts with love and tranquillity that they felt more like giving thanks than anything else. They said it was around the whole city, and some of the people were scared to death. Some said the world was on fire; some said the gods were coming down to destroy them; others said that a star had fallen; until Melker the priest came out shouting and clapping his hands, frantic with joy and told the people that the star, the angels' singing and this supernatural light which illumined the darkness of the midnight sky were signs that God was coming to fulfill His promise to Israel! That God had promised that if they would be faithful He would give them a Savior to redeem them and that He would give them eternal life! And that they should not fear, but rejoice! And he explained to them that the sign of His coming would be that light would shine from on high, and the angels would announce His coming, and their voices would be heard in the city, and a virgin that was pure should travail and bring forth her firstborn with no pain, and that He would sanctify all flesh. All of these things my father would tell us and retell us because we all liked to hear the story over and over again. *('Archko Volume'* Chapter. 4. Jonathan's interview with the Shepherds. Sanhedrim, 88 B. By R. Jose. Order No. 2)

All and all, even after such awesome angelic display and the shepherds' testimony, there were people who didn't believe that a divine birth had taken place right amongst them. My father said that Zelomi, a woman he knew who assisted births had been there, and she had told him the story of how Salome, her assistant, had doubted that Mary had given birth and that she was still a virgin after the Baby's birth. She said that when she told Salome about the wonders that she had witnessed like the angels coming out of heaven, and about the clear white light that bathed and illumined the inside of the cave, and that it appeared to be daytime in the middle of the night, Salome smiled with unbelief. But Zelomi told Salome that she should see for herself because this was the greatest miracle, that she had never seen a birth like this in which there was no blood, no sign of physical struggle, no smell of sweat or blood but on the contrary that there was an aroma inside the cave as if all the jasmines of Lebanon had sprouted; but Salome was ironic and unbelieving. At that she came to the cave and without even looking at the child went straight to Mary and said, *'Get ready, because I'm going to examine you; because there is great dissension amongst us regarding you and your virginity.'* *('Book of the infancy of the Savior'* 84)

And then she put her hand in Mary's body, but she wished she had never done so, because as soon as she touched Mary, her hand was charred as if by fire and then she screamed, *'Have pity on me! My malice and incredulity have led me to disrespect God. Because I dare to touch the living God my hand is charred and is falling from my body!'*

She says that everyone was in panic and that she wailed and cried, repenting, asking God to forgive her that she was just doing her duty trying to uncover a fraud if there would be one for the sake of the sons of Israel. Then she says that an angel came from the heavens and said to her, *'Salome, Salome, the Lord has listened to you and accepted your prayer of repentance. Come near the child, take Him in your arms and your pain will change into joy.'*

That she then went near the Baby and held him in her arms and suddenly the hand which was black and dry and threatened to fall off her body, revivified itself, and in just few instants appeared pink and even healthier than before! This was the first healing miracle that the Baby performed on this earth. Salome said that she was transfixed by the feelings inside herself and that she saw fit as soon as she came out of the cave to tell everyone of the extraordinary experience she just had. But that when she crossed the cave's threshold she was told by the angel: *'Salome, don't tell anyone of the marvels you have witnessed until the Child is in Jerusalem.'*

But Salome couldn't keep all this to herself because she was exhilarated and overwhelmed with joy and told everyone she could of the marvels that she had seen. She said that the shepherds of the region were also witnesses to that miracle and that they had also heard the choirs of angels singing and glorifying God. *('Proto Gospel of de Santiago'* 20)

And the Greek people say that when the heavenly host told the shepherds at Bethlehem of the birth of Jesus the Christ, a deep groan was heard through all the isles of Greece, because the great Pan was dead and all the royalty of Olympus was dethroned to give way to the God of Gods and His teaching of Love. And shepherd poets sang about this incident throughout their land and their poems came to our land adorned with their perception. This is one of the odes that they sang, and that we learned. It is a beautiful poem but because it is also true it makes the heart feel as if that Holy Night is springing out of your heart again and again. It goes like this,

'Peaceful was the night, wherein the Prince of Light
His reign of Peace upon the earth began
The winds, with wonder whist,
Smoothly the waters kissed,
Whispering new joys to the mild Ocean
Who for now forgot to rage,
The stars fixed in steadfast gaze
Bent to shed their precious light
On the cave, where the Babe laid asleep.
The Sun himself withheld his wonted speed
And hid his head for shame
For he saw a greater Sun appear
And his inferior flame
The new enlightened world no more should need
The shepherds heard such music sweet
Which warmed their hearts and ears

As never was by mortal finger struck
Nature, also heard the heavenly sound
And instantly knew that such harmony alone
Could hold all Heaven and Earth in bond
A globe of circular light, surrounded their sight
And with long beams the shamefaced Night arrayed;
The helmeted Cherubim
And sworded Seraphim
Glittered in light with wings spread in flight
Making such music as
Before was never made
And singing glory to all God like men,
For the redeemer of men
Will melt death from earthly mould
And Hell itself will pass away
For the new born Babe will
Open wide the gates of his high palace halls.
But not yet,
The Babe lies yet in smiling infancy
And it is on the bitter cross
That He will one day redeem our loss
From this happy day
The Old Dragon under ground
In straiter limits bound
Sees in wrath his kingdom fall.
The Oracles are dumb;
No voice or hideous hum
Runs through the arched roof in words deceiving
Apollo from his shrine
Can no more divine,
With hollow shriek the steep of Delphos leaving.
No nightly trance, or breathed spell,
Inspires the pale-eyed Priest from the prophetic cell.
The lonely Olympus over,
A voice of weeping heard and loud lament;
From haunted spring, and dale
Edged with poplar pale,
The parting Genius is with sighing sent;
The Nymphs in twilight shad of tangled thickets mourn,
Good bye Baliim and mooned Astharoth,
The gods of the Nile haste away.
But see! The Virgin blest has laid her Babe to rest
Earth outgrown the Mythic fancies

Sung beside her in her youth; And those debonair romances
Sound but dull beside the Truth.
Phoebus' chariot course is run!
Look up, poets to the Sun!
Pan is dead, Pan is dead
Long live Love, the Christ
Just born the Lord of Life!

This is a poem that we heard a thousand times! Everybody who witnessed the Miracle of His Birth told it every time they had the chance to, and in the Night when He was born, they said that they repeated it not only because its beautiful and it brings joy to the heart, but also because when they did something like a miracle happened because they seemed to live the blissful experience they had, again. So, we learned to recite it by heart just from hearing it, and on many occasions when political, or business friends of my father would come to our house, he had us recite this poem to them, when they asked about this event. My father explained to us that the changes that happened were registered all over the earth and the sky, and that there were wise men that traveled from afar to worship the Babe for they knew how to read the sky. They say that there were many wonders and that the shepherds who witnessed His birth were completely changed. Everybody that saw them, or spoke with them said they were *'Heaven touched.'* And that when the oldest one died he was not afraid, but happy to go to the heavenly realm that He had seen that night, and that he asked to be buried in Shepherds' Field at the site where the angels had come to talk to them.

At night, when all was quiet and we went to bed my father used to ask Martha and I what story we would like to hear, to help us to have a good experience in the land of dreams. Invariably both of us wanted to hear stories about Baby-Jesus, but we loved specially the story of that Holy Night in which the Heavens opened and legions of angels came down from its vaults, to celebrate with men that their Savior had been born. There was a special magic to the story of that night when the earth was made Holy. . . It seemed to me that when I closed my eyes and I asked Jesus to keep me forever in that place of light where He lives. . . It became alive. . . And I could see and hear the angels singing a lullaby for all children to sleep in peace and never again fear the darkness of the night. And since that day, we celebrated that Holy Night every year, as everyone in the Essene community did. The shepherds came to our house and to many other houses and retold children the story of the Holy birth, afterwards we all shared a special meal with many people and the head of the household always had presents for all in remembrance of the great generosity of God who had given us that Holy Night, His greatest gift, His own Son.   The birth of Jesus was always a special day in all of our lives, and from then on this Holy Night when God willed to become one of us started to be called a day of celebration of Love's Birth.   And that is where the word Christmas comes from, because the word Christ means power of Love and the word Mass means celebration and since that time until this day that Holy Night is celebrated by all who love Jesus and want to be part of His Kingdom of Love.   So from now on when you say *'Merry Christmas'* let your heart sing and know that you are saying *'Be Happy and Celebrate Love!'*   It was hard to have favorite stories when they were about Jesus; they were all full of magic and of something so special, which I can't compare to any other tale.   This story was like a flood of peace and love pouring in my heart, just like if someone was giving a gentle massage to my heart, it was easy to just let go into that feeling which permeated that Holy Night and drift peacefully into sleep. . .

I would like to share another story that also happened about the time when Baby Jesus was just born and that I was told because of my kitty-cat's markings.   I have a kitty-cat, his name is *'Sun-Face'* because his face looks like a sunrise, he is a gold colored kitty-cat with white muzzle, and paws that make him look as if he is wearing white gloves and boots and he has an *'M'* marking on its forehead.   One day, Rachel, the shepherdess who brings fresh milk to our house everyday, saw my kitty-cat and she asked me, *'Do you know how the Tabby cats got the 'M' they wear on their forehead?'*

And I said, *'No, I think it was always his, it was born with it.'*

Then Rachel said,   *'Well, I tell you, that who gave all kitty-cats of its kind the right to wear the 'M' on their foreheads was Mary, the mother of the God-child that was born in Bethlehem.   And if you want to hear the story, I will tell it to you because nobody can tell it better than I do, because it happened to be that I was there. . .'*

My eyes and mouth opened as big as they could out of surprise and delight and I asked intrigued, *'Could you tell me the story now? Please, do.'* And Rachel sat me on her lap and told me this story, and this is what she said, *'The name of the story is. . . Let's see. . .*

How the Tabby Cat got the 'M' That They Wear on Their Forehead.

It happened that a few days after the Divine Child was born I had gone to the cave where He and His family were staying, to bring some fresh milk for Joseph and Mary. When I came into the cave, the Baby was crying and they said that He had been crying incessantly and nobody knew why, because Baby Jesus never cried before. And they didn't know what to do to calm Him down. The angels of heaven who brought daily to Baby Jesus His heavenly food, had already fed Him. Some of them were present and played heavenly music for Him, but the Baby continued to cry.

The ox and the mule that lived in the cave got as close as they could to the manger to warm it. Mary took the Baby in her arms so that He was clean and freshened and then walked Him up and down, while Salome made the manger more comfortable for Him. When she had finished doing this, Mary put the Baby back on the manger and gave Him a kiss, but He continued to cry. A cousin of mine, who visits the cave everyday since that night divine in which He was born played a beautiful song with the flute, and two of his sheep who were around the cave and looked concerned about the Baby's crying came into the cave and said, *'Beeeeeee' 'Beeeeeeeee'* trying to help, but the Baby continued to cry. Mary and I sang to Him a lullaby, without any success. The dog of another shepherd seeing that the sheep's singing didn't help came into the cave also and went *'Woof' 'Woof'* but despite its best intentions, the Baby continued to cry.

A cow that was feeding itself in a pasture near the cave came in when it heard the crying and went *'Moooooooo' 'Mooooooooo'* hoping that her singing would stop the Baby's cry, but it didn't help, for He continued to cry. We were at a loss and no one knew what to do. And then, the most wonderful thing happened!

16

The kitty cat wanted to come up to see the Baby, but it was shy and small, so he had been hiding in a corner.

My cousin the shepherd, has a kitty cat, which he had brought to the cave for he wanted Baby Jesus to bless it. The kitty cat wanted to come up to see the Baby, but it was small and shy, so he had been hiding in a corner hoping that someone would notice it and help him up. My cousin's kitty cat is cuddly and friendly as yours is, but there were too many people and too much noise so he didn't dare to come out. My cousin stood near it and noticed that the kitty cat rubbed itself on his leg and said *'Meow,' 'Meow'* and looked at him as if it wanted help to come near the Baby and do his try. He picked up the kitty cat and put it on the manger near Baby Jesus, so that it would warm Him up because the air was somewhat brisk and the kitty cat rolled itself as a little fur ball next to the Baby and started to *'Purrrrr'* and *'Purrrr.'* In that instant the Baby stopped crying and smiled. He blessed the one that had been forgotten and looked at all of us as if He was saying, *'At last, you understood!'* Pretty soon the only sound one could hear in the cave was the soothing sound of the kitty cat's *'Purrrrrr'* and the only thing one could feel was the breath of both the Baby and the kitty-cat. . . The Baby felt the softness of the kitty cat's fur with His hands and with a smile went to sleep. . . And all was quiet and we all felt an overwhelming Peace in our hearts. . .

17

Mary feeling grateful for such a nice and warm presence said to the kitty cat, *'I give you the 'M' of my name as a token of thank you from my Son and I for bringing your soft and quiet nature to the cave and warming up my Baby. From now on you and all your kind will be marked on your forehead with the first letter of my name, so that everyone knows that you and your kind are close to my heart.'*

And in that very moment, as if by magic, the *'M'* of *'Mary'* appeared on the kitty cat's forehead! And this is why since that day, all of its kind wears it as a symbol of their kinship with Mary and Jesus. So, now you know why your kitty cat has an *'M'* on its forehead. And the crux of the story is that Baby Jesus knew that the kitty cat wanted to be near Him, but because it was too shy to come on his own it was still waiting in a corner for someone to remember it and bring it to Him to be blessed, but everyone had forgotten it. So, Baby Jesus cried until someone brought the kitty cat near Him. Did you like my story? I bet you did; I can see it in your happy face! Do you want me to tell it again? *'Ah!'* Rachel said, *'There is one more thing you will like to know, and that is that other cats know this story for they have collective intelligence. So, what one knows, all the others know immediately. So, all other cats always bow in front of 'Tabby cats' because they know that those felines who wear the 'M' like a crown on their heads are special in Mary's heart. And don't let anybody tell you that this is just a story, for I, Rachel was in that cave and saw how the 'M' appeared on the first 'Tabby's forehead.'*

And I gave Rachel a big thank you kiss on her cheek, because since that day I look at my kitty cat with different eyes! For *'Sun Face'* wears his *'M,'* such a precious gift, as the one its kind received from Mary the Mother of God and Queen of the Angels, without pride, in silence and humility. And when it purrs I also feel the peace of the beautiful and gentle company of my silent friend and pet that made Baby Jesus feel at home and I am happy.

In some of the stories I know about the flight to Egypt, Baby Jesus did portents and wonders, magic things which helped the situation they found themselves in, as only God himself can do. Hearing these tales was second to being there, I could see with my mind. . . So I asked my father to repeat these stories to me again and again until I fell asleep, because this way I felt that I was part of the story and that little Jesus was with me. . . So I had wonderful dreams which sometimes were a literal continuation of the stories. . . My father said that during their flight to Egypt, the Archangel Gabriel gave the care of the divine Baby and Mary to a small group, these were Joseph, his sons and Melker the wise man and his servants, who had prepared a caravan to travel from Tibet to Egypt. It ostensibly looked simply as a merchant's caravan, but its true object was to provide safe and comfortable transit into Egypt to its precious cargo. Lucky people those who went with them! My parents had offered their services to Melker, who was in charge of the caravan, but he told them that they couldn't go in a big group because they couldn't call attention on themselves. My father told us that in spite of having taken this precaution, when the caravan got near the border of Egypt, the soldiers of Herod came close to Mary and the Baby and would have killed Him, had not Melker used his mystical power* to dematerialize Mary and the Baby, who immediately materialized again after they left. I felt that if I had been older I would have gone too! But Martha, who was almost three years older than I didn't even get to go, so maybe they wouldn't have allowed me to go either.

Note* The practice of this power is well known in India today, where the mystics do not abuse, but use to not make arduous trips across the jungles or impassable roads, on foot, except for some special purpose.

Martha, John, my little brother, and I grew up hearing my father tell many stories about Baby Jesus. He would tell us of how He made miracles and prodigies who stirred up the town folks, and how these were sometimes frightened of his powers, and said that He was a magician, because they did not understand that His Nature was Divine. We all loved these stories! But I loved especially the one about their arrival to Egypt. I went like this. . .

They said that after many hours of traveling, the small caravan of the Baby-God arrived in Egypt. Mary, fatigued as a consequence of the long journey from Bethlehem, wanted to rest and Archangel Gabriel, who was always guarding them, directed the group to the area of the Great Pyramids, and Mary fascinated with the Sphinx, went towards it and admired it. And she felt that it was a perfect place to shelter the Baby and herself from the night desert chill and the wind, so she climbed on it and found between its paws a perfect place to sleep. So, she put the Baby in her lap and immediately went to sleep.

It happened that some desert thieves had seen the caravan. And seeing the radiance that the Baby exuded, which could be clearly seen from the distance, thought, as thieves always think, that the radiance was that of a rich treasure of gold or diamonds shining under the light of the stars; and they said to each other,

'How lucky we are, for this is certainly a very rich merchant carrying lots of gold and diamonds, or a huge diamond! For what else could cause this radiance under the stars, but a thing of such nature?'

They got closer and seeing Mary asleep felt that it was a good time to rob the treasure that she had on her lap, which they could not see well due to the radiance. But as they got closer, they saw that the light was coming out of a Baby and that He was not asleep, but looking at them. The thieves didn't mind the Baby, because they were now entranced with the beauty of the sleeping lady who was more enticing to them than the diamonds that at first they had envisioned to steal and continued to get closer to her. . .

When the Baby saw their intention He lifted His little hand and with His index finger pointed at the Sphinx. . . At this, Harmachis opened up its secret chamber and the Baby and His Mother disappeared right in front of the eyes of the startled thieves!

Once Mary and Baby Jesus had disappeared, the Sphinx erected itself menacing growing in size and darkness in front of the unbelieving eyes of the thieves!

The ominous image of Harmachis, known to the desert Bedouins as, *'The Mother of Terrors'* threw the thieves down on the sand shaking of fear. Trembling, they got on their knees as they could, and swore to Harmachis by their lives that if she spared their lives they would never steal anything again.

The next morning they begged Mary and the Baby for forgiveness. The divine Baby smiled at them and signaled towards Melker, they understood and implored Melker to take them as his servants and students, for they wanted to learn from his wisdom and to serve the wonder Baby, who had looked at them and changed their hearts. Feiliexus and Heirsleus, for those were their names, were allowed to stay.

And the caravan continued their journey until they reached their destination. This was the region of the three mountains where the *'Therapeutas'* or the Egyptian Essene community had its center and Joseph, Mary and the Baby lived until Archangel Gabriel let them know that it was safe to come back to Palestine.

I tell these stories of my childhood memories because many children who love Jesus have never been told these stories of His babyhood, or of His childhood. They were so important in my life. For they helped me to know Jesus and to understand better His divine nature and powers. I want to share what I know with other children that they may profit, as I did, from knowing all the wonders that Jesus did when He was a child. I also would like to have the grown-ups see how silly they can be sometimes, when they deny what they do not understand. One of my favorite stories happened when they were first fleeing to Egypt. . . Jesus was not even a year old.

My father says that one day. . . The small caravan which escorted the Baby, Joseph, Mary and few young lads, had left behind Gaza, which is about forty Roman miles from Jerusalem, from there on the road to the delta is long and there aren't many places to replenish water and food for the road. After they had left behind the last Jewish

City, they came to the proximity of one of the many desert grottos on the road and Mary wanted to stop to rest there for a while. So, she took the sleeping Baby in her arms, came down from the cart and placed Baby-Jesus on her lap. But to the horror of Joseph and Mary some snake dragons came out whistling from the cave looking very threatening, their aspect was horrible and with their whistles and open jaws they would terrify anyone. Joseph, Mary and the young lads of their company were frozen in place! Then to everyone's surprise, Baby Jesus opened His eyes, came down from Mary's lap and stood in front of the snake and the dragons. The animals retreated a little, bowed in front of Jesus and went back in silence into the darkest part of the cave. Mary and Joseph were still in shock, but Jesus calmed them down at the same time that He ordered the reptiles to not harm anyone. (*'Gospel of Pseudo Mathew'* 18.)

I loved this story the best because like my father explained to us; it showed that Baby Jesus, even when He apparently was just a small baby, was the one protecting those who seemed to be His protectors. Because He is God and all of nature obeys His command, no matter how ferocious they may appear to us. It made me feel that if Baby Jesus was around, nothing could harm my sister, or I, not even the bad king Herod. So, as I did always when it got dark, I asked him to come into my crib and sleep with me, and I would feel the Baby coming into my crib with me, and then His mother would come and cover the two of us with her blue mantle full of stars. . . And I would fear no more.

So, I grew up feeling that He would always be there if I needed Him. One day, much later in life I was going to see that my childhood's instincts were correct. Usually before I fell asleep I took advantage of my father's patience and when He would finish telling the story I asked him to tell the story again and again. . . Until I fell asleep. My father said that this story was also a favorite of his, but sometimes he felt that all the stories he heard about Jesus were his favorites! I felt he loved Him and his parents in a special way. As far as I am concerned I had many, many favorite stories. . . All of them!

Another of these desert stories that I love is the one of the Palm tree. The story says that Baby Jesus and His people were on the way to Egypt and they decided to stop and rest. They were all tired because the sun and the dry air in the desert are very hard when there's no breeze, and this was one of those days. And Mary saw a palm tree with good shade and sat to rest under it. Joseph put the cart next to the palm tree and helped Mary to come down from the donkey. She was very thirsty and hungry, so, when she looked up to the palm tree and saw it full of wonderful dates she said to Joseph, *'If it were possible, I would love to eat some dates.'*

Joseph responded that the palm tree was too high and that he didn't think he could reach them, and that he was more concerned about their water supply because it was very scarce. Then the Baby, who was resting in his mother's lap said to the palm tree,

'Bend down, palm tree, and give your fruits to my mother.'

And the palm tree bent down all the way to Mary's feet. Mary took its fruits and gave some to Joseph and the Baby. The palm tree stayed bent until Baby Jesus ordered it to go back to its normal position and said to it, **'The water that circulates in your veins would help us. Make it surface from the soil so that we can drink and refill our water canteen.'**

And in that instant water sprang out of the roots of the palm tree in a stream of fresh and pristine water, so that everyone, including the animals, could quench their thirst!

We tried to talk to the palm tree to see if it would obey us too, but it didn't. My father explains everything to us, so when we asked him why didn't the Palm tree obey us, he said that it is because Jesus is Love, and Love is the essence of everything there is, so everything, even the stones know His voice, as this story shows. And he added, seeing our amazed expressions, everything in the world, even if we think it's inanimate, knows and obeys the Baby for He is the Word of God, Love Itself

Next morning, when they were ready to leave the Baby said to the palm tree, *'I will give you a privilege palm tree: one of your branches will be transported by one of my angels and will be planted in Paradise. And from now on, you will be the sign of triumph in earth, in such a way that whomever triumphs would receive the palm of victory.'*

And they say that in that moment appeared an angel from heaven, who took a palm tree branch and transported it to Paradise. Everyone who witnessed this event prostrated themselves in the floor and were overwhelmed with fear. Jesus calmed them down telling them, *'Don't fear. This palm, transported to Paradise, will be for all of you a remembrance of the victory that awaits humanity.'*

My father says that when he heard these stories he felt hopeful for humanity, seeing that if the plants and the beasts respond to Love, and are in peace with each other, maybe humans would start to do the same. And to illustrate the wisdom of animals, father told a beautiful story. It is said, that as soon as the little caravan of Baby Jesus, came into Egypt, the lions and leopards natural to the region, came to them out of their caves and led the little group by roads in which there were no thieves, or people who could harm them.

The people who witnessed the event said that it was unbelievable the way that the Baby communicated with the big cats and assured His parents that there was no cause for fear in front of them. These people said that they had never in their lives seen anything like it, that after talking with the animals, Baby Jesus told His parents that the lions and leopards would walk next to the donkey and that the donkey wouldn't mind, and that it was so. The donkey was perfectly tranquil walking besides the big cats, as if they were sheep or another animal of their kind! The cats seemed to be very happy to serve the little caravan as guides and behaved in an uncommonly friendly manner.

'And the wolf shall graze with the sheep, and the lion shall lie with the ox.'

My father says that there is a prophecy of Isaiah which says that the wolf shall graze with the sheep and the lion and the calf will lay together in the straw and that this story made Him think of that. There are many, many stories of the journey through the desert, I wish I could tell them all, but that would require more paper and more time than it is available on earth, some of these stories are about curing the deaf and the dumb, of people possessed of evil spirits that were freed just by the presence of Jesus in the town, of lepers that healed when they touched the water with which Mary had washed Jesus' clothes. So many, so many wonders that He did and that we do not know. . .

So, He took a dry fish, put it in the Nile dipped His hands in the water and ordered it to swim! Then the fish shook off the salt and was as alive as if it had never been dry!

When Jesus was two years old they were living in a small town near the Nile in the house of a widow. On one occasion He was seeing other children play and he wanted to join them. So, He took a dry fish, put it in the Nile dipped His hands in the water and ordered it to swim! And the fish did so! Then the fish shook off the salt and was as alive as if it had never been dry! But an old neighbor observed what happened and started telling all the people that the widow harbored a magician in her house and the widow was forced to tell them to go and they had to move to another town.

These sort of things were happening to them constantly, Joseph and Mary suffered seeing how people reacted to Jesus and they were looking forward to go back to Galilee. Some grown-ups either disbelieved, or feared the wonders of Baby Jesus, I could not understand why. If God can create tree out of seeds, and man, and whole universes out of star dust, and star dust out of just His Will, as my father says He does, the stories about the wonders of God should not be so difficult to believe.

It is not difficult for us to believe in the wonders and miracles of God even if He appears to be a Baby, maybe because my father explained them well. . . I don't understand why people could be frightened of the Baby-God. . . Maybe grown ups are afraid of the things they make up in their minds. . .

I would advise them to stop measuring God with their own ruler. As for myself, He was my Hero, I think I loved Baby Jesus, before I ever knew how to love, and the stories about Him were more enchanting to me than fairy tales. Mary His Mother, told my father a story about Jesus and John His cousin that shows His love for everyone and the perfection of His actions, even when He was a child.

On a certain occasion Jesus broke into tears without any apparent reason. He rarely cried and His face was so sad that His mother was very concerned and asked Him if there was something really bad happening, and Jesus answered, *'I cry because your cousin Elizabeth has left this world and John is alone. He is now alone on the mountain and he's crying over her dead body.'* When she heard this Mary was so sad, she herself began to cry anguished to think of little John alone in the desert caves, where they had been hiding from Herod's wrath. When Jesus saw her crying, He forgot His pain and in order to console Mary, He told her that He would get her where John and Elizabeth were. And in that instant Jesus lifted His little hand up to the sky and called a cloud to come down. The cloud obedient descended to the earth, flying down as if it was a bird and landed where they were. Mary and Jesus climbed onto it and were transported with swiftness and softness to the desert of Qumran where John was. They embraced him and consoled John, and they washed the body of Elizabeth and buried it.

Mary wanted to take John with them, but Jesus stopped her saying, *'That is not my Father's wish. John will stay in the desert until the appointed moment. But do not fear: Gabriel one of my archangels will take care of John, and will feed him and protect him until the time of his mission comes.'*

Jesus then gave His cousin a little shell from the Ocean, which He endowed with a special quality.

Then, Jesus gave orders to Archangel Gabriel, who was His own personal guardian angel, to care for John. At this, a host of baby angels flew down from heaven that had been appointed by Gabriel to keep company to John for as long as he remained in the desert. And John was now at peace. Then Baby Jesus then gave His cousin a little shell from the Ocean which He endowed with a special quality, so that whenever John felt hungry he just had to pick up some sand with it, and the sand would turn into whatever food he needed at the moment.

After this, they embraced and said farewell for both children knew well that they were not going to see each other for a long time. At that moment the cloud came down again and took Mary and Jesus back to Egypt.

Children can understand these stories about Jesus. They can understand that there is nothing impossible for Him, and that He taught people to be better without words, and created beautiful, living things whenever He wanted. I never had a problem; neither did the other children I knew. The only thing was that when I had dreams I didn't know if these stories I dream were more or less real than the ones that were happening far away from me. Sometimes when my father told a story of Baby-Jesus I felt that I had been there, they were all so real to me!

My father enjoyed telling us the new stories that he had heard about Jesus, as much as we loved hearing them, so we heard many, many stories, of course we all wanted to meet Him and be near Him! We asked father if it would be possible, and he said that we would and maybe sooner than we expected!

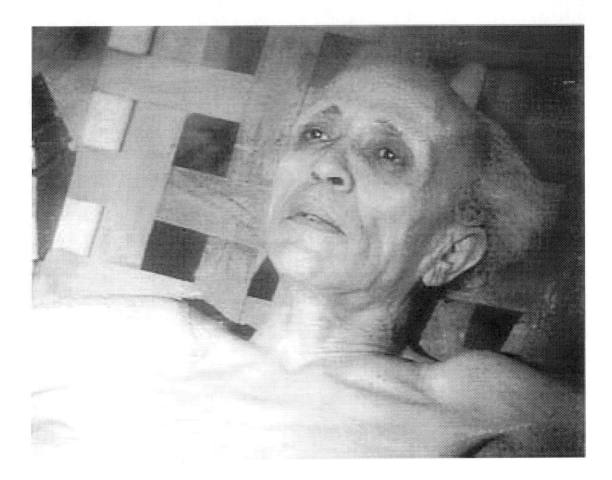

Herod, the bad king had died eaten by worms that came out from his own body, an illness, that not even the baths of Callirroe could alleviate.

One day when I was about three years old. . . A friend of my father came home and told him that Herod, the bad king had died eaten by worms that came out from his own body, an illness, that not even the baths of Callirroe could alleviate. So there was no more danger and we all could go back to Palestine. He said that Herod was so cruel and evil that before he died he had his own son Antipatro killed, and also three hundred of the most distinguished citizens of Palestine because he wanted the mourning for his death to be felt by all. I clapped my hands of content for the news of his death, and Martha said I was not a good girl and that I should say a prayer for him. I must not be a good girl because even after she said that to me, I felt good that he had died.

32

Well, few days after we had gotten the news of the bad king's death, our father called us and said that Archangel Gabriel had come to Joseph and directed them to go back to Galilee, where they should go and live in En-Nazira, a small settlement around a spring. The happy news were that the Holy Family were on their way back, and our home happened to be on their route, so, they would be staying with us for a few days!

It was exactly the time of my birthday! Jesus the miracle Baby and His parents were going to stay in our home for few days!

The three of us started jumping and asking the angels to help us to be the best friends for them. And we sang twirling and twirling around and around,

'Angels from above, (raising the arms up)
And angels from below, (with the arms down)
Please show us how to offer the best hospitality to the Baby God! (Twirling and
turning clockwise)
Angels from above, (raising the arms up)
And angels from below, (with the arms down)
Hear us and tell us everythint we need to know'! ! (Twirling and turning counter-
clockwise)

After we calmed down my father said that we should be very nice, that he expected us to be good hosts for them and to be mindful and considerate because they needed rest after their journey. He said that the parents of Jesus were happy to stay with us before they went back to Palestine and that the greatest of all blessing was to be near the Child. I will never forget that day. . . ! It was as if God had given me the best birthday present a child could hope for! Jesus was going to be staying with us! Have you ever had a dream come true? That's how it felt!

The day they arrived even the Sun seemed to shine in a special way.

That was my first kiss. . . ! And one that I would never be able to forget!

The day they arrived to our home we were all excited, yet my father had reminded us to be gentle and considerate because they had been traveling, and desert traveling is very exhausting, so the three of us were very good and quiet. It was a day where all the flowers of our garden were in bloom and it seemed to me that there were more butterflies and birds than ever, even the Sun seemed to shine in a special way. At last we were all going to meet them, Jesus and Mary his mother!

Martha and I had put flowers everywhere! We had made a path with rose petals and candles, so that they would know which was our house when they arrived no matter if it was day or night. And we made a sign for the doorway saying to them how happy we were to have them stay with us. All of a sudden we saw them! As they approached our house they became more and more real, they were not just a magical and beautiful story or a dream anymore, but they were flesh and blood, just as one of us. When I saw Jesus I thought that I was going to die of love! I felt as if I was wrapped in warmth from head to toes as I used to feel when my mother was alive and hugged me. I was so happy to see Him in person; He was just as I had imagined Him to be! I think that this is when I fell in love with Him. He was wearing a caftan and the man's typical headgear for the desert and looked like a little desert prince! He was so luminous and beautiful! Mary was also beautiful and very young! But Jesus was like the sun, I could not take my eyes from him! I have no words to say what He was like to me! The first thing He did was to embrace each one of us and give us a big kiss! That was my first kiss. . . And one that I would never be able to forget!

When they came into the house we remember our father's advice and allowed them to make themselves comfortable. We offered them water and towels to wash their feet and also offered them some food and fruits and goat cheese from our goats. Our mother had died when Lazarus was born, so Mary wanted to help the servants to prepare the meal and she and Martha picked flowers for the table. She brought to our home that presence and the love of the mother that we all missed. After dinner the adults were talking and Jesus wanted to play.

When we played Jesus and Lazarus played like two brothers and I was always Lazarus' playmate, so I ended up being very close to Jesus too. Martha who was the older one took care of Lazarus, Jesus and I, so, we all had lots of fun.   There was no way to be bored with Him.

Jesus would do wonders and fun things, one day we went to the well that supplied water for the city and he broke all the water jugs that our mothers had given us to bring water back to them, and He threw them into the well, a girl who didn't know Jesus started crying afraid of being punished by her parents.

And Jesus said, *'Don't cry, we are just playing, the well will give us the jugs back!'*

And Jesus gave orders to the well and the water rose all the way up to the border and gave each one of us our jugs back, but full of fresh water that glittered under the sun as if it was made of light!

Another day we went to play under the shadow of a gigantic tree. Jesus gave orders to it to bend down and the tree did so and offered its branches. Then, Jesus climbed on and ordered the tree to straighten itself up, and it did so! Jesus was up above it, and could see far away, and He was telling us of all the things that He could see and we couldn't, because we were not able to climb as high up as He was. And He was there for about an hour telling us all these things that He could see, until I got frustrated because I couldn't see anything and I shouted to Him, *'Jesus, you are up there and you can see all these things, but we cannot see anything! We also want to see! Why don't you order the tree to come down and pick us up, so that we also can come up and see what you see!'*

And He laugh as He answered me, *'You could have come up an hour ago, if you would have only asked me then! Why didn't you ask before? Ask and you will have wonderful things happen to you!'* Then, he ordered the tree to bend down and we all went up and were really happy seeing everything and everyone from up high.

On another occasion Jesus, Lazar and other boys were playing with mud near a creek. It was a Sabbath day. Jesus was busy making twelve little birds of mud. A neighbor who happened to pass by, got upset because he felt that the child was working with mud and violating the Sabbath, so he went to Joseph and said, *'Your son is near the creek and he is working the mud, with that he is violating the Sabbath law'* Joseph came to the creek and reprimanded Jesus in front of all the other children. Jesus didn't pay too much attention, neither he answered Joseph, but instead He talked to the little clay birds and said,

'Fly! Fly away!'

In that instant, the clay figures became lovely sparrows full of life that started chirping and took off flying! (*'Book of the Infancy of the Savior'* Ms. Lat. 11867 Paris 1 De Santos 221)

The children who saw this were excited and when they got home, they told the story to their parents, but the grown-ups, as I said before are very, very strange, when they heard the story, they prohibited their children to play with Jesus, *'Do not play with him because he is a dangerous magician.'* They told them, *'He is like the Ne-neferka-Path magician, who used to take mud from the river and make boats with paddles which he would put in the Nile with a spell to make them appear to be alive and rowing by themselves.'*

But the children were not afraid of Jesus; on the contrary, they were enchanted and wanted to play with Him more than ever. Martha, Lazarus and I talked about this situation, our father is not like them, we definitely do not understand some grown-ups, and we feel very lucky to have the father we have. When one of them asks me, what would I like to be when I grow up? I tell them, *'A child, because I see that it is not too much fun to be a grown-up, think or do the things they do.'*

I tell them that, because sometimes they do awful things to their children; once the father of one of Jesus' friends, locked his son up in a room with a very high and small window, so small it was that only a light ray could come in! He did that terrible thing to his son, so that he couldn't go to play with Jesus, and the child was crying and asked Jesus to help him out. Jesus said to the child,

'Get your hand out! But the child couldn't do it, because the window was too small for it, then Jesus said, 'or at least a finger!'

The child did this, and Jesus took his finger and slipped the whole child through that small opening and they went to play. After they had finished playing, He slipped him back into the room with the same method. All of these things He did. It seemed that nothing was impossible for Him!

This same parent, who was the major among the Pharisees and the Scribes, went to Joseph complaining about Jesus. He was upset because Jesus had done such wonders that the children were looking up to Him as a demigod; and, angered said, *'Take a look at our children, amongst whom I include my son, they follow Jesus everywhere, even to the field of Sychar!'*

Irate because Joseph could not see any wrong doing, he took a stick with all the intention of beating up Jesus, and he followed the children until they came to the skirt of a mountain. He hid there waiting for the right moment to strike his blow and when he saw Jesus he went to hit him. . . Jesus seeing that took a jump from the top of the mountain to a spot that was as distant as the throw of an arrow. Then, all the other kids tried to do the same, and they fell off the cliff and broke their necks, arms and legs. But Jesus cured them all and left them even healthier than they were before.

Seeing all this, the archisynagoguo, bowed in front of Jesus and acknowledged that God was with Him. There is a place in Sychar, which even today is called *'The Lord's Jump'* in memory of this incident.

On another occasion, all of us kids were walking near Rachel's tomb, which is between Bethlehem and Jerusalem. It was the time for sowing, and Jesus saw a man in the fields who was sowing chick peas, and He asked the man,
'What are you sowing?'

And the man said, *'What do you think? Stones!'*

And Jesus said, **'Be it as you have said, from now on you will reap what you sow, stones.'**

And all the chickpeas this man had sowed became really hard stones.   If you look carefully, even today, you can find small stones in that area near Rachel's tomb, the little stones have the shape and the color of chickpeas, and even the dent.

Jesus, was the hero of our playmates and definitely my brother's, my sister's and I. He brought us children, the joy of unlimited experiences to our lives, the true essence of childhood. Jesus helped us to enjoy just being children and to see how limited many of the adults had become, because they have forgotten how to see with the heart, they measure everything with their own measure, think too much and feel not. In other words, they have forgotten to *'just be,'* wrapped as they were in their daily tasks and toil to have this or that. Later on, Jesus was going to say **'In order to enter into the Kingdom of Heaven, you must become as a child.'**

On another occasion, we were going to play and we found two Roman soldiers having a fight. And Jesus said to us, **'Let's sit and watch them,'** so we did.

One of the soldiers became self-conscious when he saw us sitting there in silence watching them argue, and looking at Jesus, he said, *'Child, where are you from? And where are you going? What are you doing here? And what is your name?'*

And Jesus replied, **'If I answer your question with the truth, you will not be able to comprehend.'**

But the soldier didn't give up and asked Jesus again, Tell me, *'Is your father alive? And your mother?'*

And Jesus responded to him, **'In fact my Father is alive and is immortal, and my Mother is part of Him.'**

Then the soldier said, *'What! Immortal?'*

And Jesus replied, **'Yes, immortal, He was before anything you know began, and death has no power over Him.'**

Then the soldier said, *'Who is such a one that is immortal and over who death has no power, being that you say that he has immortality assured?'*

And Jesus said, **'You would not be able to know Him, nor even to have an approximate idea of Him.'**

Then the soldier asked, *'Who is able to?'*

And Jesus said, **'No one.'**

Then the soldier intrigued asked, *'Where is your father's dwelling?'*

And Jesus responded, **'In Heaven.'**

Then the soldier said, *'In Heaven above the earth? How can you then go home and be with him?'*

Then Jesus said, *'I am from Heaven, and as a matter of fact, even now I am in Heaven and with Him.'*

Then the soldier said, *'I am not able to comprehend what you are talking about.'*

And Jesus said to him, *'I told you so at the beginning of our conversation, for my Father is Ineffable and Inexplicable.'*

Then the soldier asked, *'Who then, can comprehend?'*

And Jesus said, *'If your desire to know is strong and from your heart, not from your mind and you beg me, I will give you the grace to Understand.'*

And the soldier genuflecting and bowing his head in front of the child said, *'Nino Dio, explain this mystery to me.'*

And Jesus explained to him about the eternal generation of life of His Father and about the temporal generation in the virginal womb of His Mother. . . Things that we don't understand, but that in a way we know to be true, even if we don't know why. Then He closed the eyes of the soldier with His little hands and made him see the Light that never dies. . . And the soldier left a changed man and we all marveled at the way that he spoke with the adults. And we asked Jesus why had He shown these things to this man, and He said that when He sat to watch them argue, He knew that this man was ready *'to Know Him.'* (Syriac text from the *'Arab Gospels of the Infancy of Jesus'.' I. Daietsy'* vol. A and B in the collection Of the Mequitaristas of Venice. *'Ankano girkh Nor Ketakar anatz'*)

Our household was always happy because there was abundance and my father gave to others who didn't have and there was also a lot of love, but the stay of the Holy Family in our home brought something more to all of us. Martha was in heaven! She became very close to Mary, who was only nine years older than she was. Lazarus found in Jesus the brother that he never had and was happier than ever. As for me, I fell in love with Jesus as soon as I saw Him and since that moment my life became alive and magic! One day, one of my father's friends said that He and I reminded him of the Greek statues of the child Cupid and Psyche, for we loved each other as only children, or angels know how to love. And he teased me saying that maybe we would get married one day soon. But I was serious, for to me that was not something I wanted to joke about. I knew well that people do not get married that young and I kept my love secretly guarded in my heart. Many other friends of ours came to play and meet Jesus, they all wanted to have Him as a friend, and all of our friends had more fun around Him than they ever had and we all wished they would have stayed with us forever! It was in this epoch when Jesus walked on a ray of sunlight! We were playing in a room that had a really high ceiling. It was afternoon and the sun had gone down a little; the window was half closed and by the opening a single ray of sunlight was shining making like a luminous path inside the room. Jesus said to us, *'Who dares to embrace this ray of sunlight and climb up on it?'*

Nobody answered. Then Jesus embraced the sunray with his arms and climbed up on it to the upper part of the window! We were all so amazed! One by one we all tried to do it, but no one was able to embrace the sunray because it would slip into nothing when we tried to catch it! We laughed so much, all took turns trying and had a lot of fun seeing that it wasn't as easy as it seemed.

And He said to us, *'Is not that difficult to climb a sunray, but you cannot do it because you believe that you can't. You have forgotten how.'* When the children came back to their homes they told their parents of the wonders that Jesus could do, but the parents were not happy about it.   (*'Armenian Gospel from the Infancy of Jesus'* 15, 5)

They asked my father if it was true what the children were saying, and He calmed them down, but Mary felt that once again they might turn against Jesus.

This was mainly the reason that they left our home. Because Joseph was afraid that if more people would hear about the incidents of Jesus walking on the sunray and the other prodigies He did things could get complicated, and after all, they also needed to be on their way to En-Nazir. When Jesus left I felt as if the sun, the moon and all the stars had been taken out of heaven and they would never shine again. . . At least until I saw Him again. Now He is gone and who knows for how long! I would have liked to go with Him, but I can't for I am just a small child. Sometimes it is sad to be a child and not be able to make your dreams come true, like the adults can.

Bethany

View from the upper terrace of the house in Bethany, far in the horizon, where the Sun is born, one can see the Dead Sea.'

Soon after the Holy Family's departure, we also left Egypt, we were going to live in Bethany near Jerusalem, and I had mixed emotions about leaving Egypt. I loved Egypt!

My father used to take us for boat rides on the Nile. In numerous occasions when we passed by Giza, he would anchor the boat right in front of the Pyramids and the great Sphinx. Then, he would tell us about the mysteries that were hidden in those vaults and of how the birth and the end of the Adamic race and the mission of salvation of Jesus was written in those stones. . .

My child's imagination would run free. . . And the most incredible things happened to me! I could see things from another time. . . One day I saw myself as an Egyptian Queen. . . Taking two black panthers for a walk in the desert at night. . . Another time I saw myself going into the Sphinx's temple. . . There were servants following me with peacock feather fans, which they moved rhythmically to scare away the flying insects. . . And the Hierophant coming to greet me. . . This other reality was as real to me as the current one, maybe that's why I always felt when my father would talk about the Egyptian mysteries that I had first hand knowledge of what he was talking about. It was as if I had all that knowledge stored inside me and all he was doing was refreshing it. I felt that at that time I had known all the secrets of the universe and I had forgotten them because of a collective misuse of that knowledge which plunged us into a very deep darkness. Yet, even when I had not even a faint memory of what I used to know, I knew that I have known what everything is.

Maybe that's why I felt that I belonged here in Egypt. I felt that Egypt was an integral part of me and I knew that some day I was going to be back. It was sad for me to say good-bye to Egypt. It was as if part of me, that was part of a greater mystery than the sensory world, was closing shut for me.

The house my father bought for us was up on the hills of Bethany Shia. The house was on the top of a mountain full of olive and orange trees, whose blossoms perfumed the air. At night the sound of silence and of myriad of crickets who pierce it in sporadic spurts of that particular sound they make, could be heard like a concert of thousands of little bells played by musicians one can hear but never see. . . This house is in Judea, very near Jerusalem. Later on, it was going to become the place where Jesus rested when He was in the area. . . I often wonder if my father chose to live in this area and bought this house with that specific purpose. He doesn't tell us much about the link that he has with his Essene brothers and what they know about Jesus, but I know that he knows things that he doesn't tell anyone.

Before we went to Egypt my parents used to live in Magadal Nunya on the shore of Lake Gennesereth, a beautiful and rich city that is situated between Caphernaum and Tiberias. My father liked Galilee, but when we were in Egypt my mother died and he sold the house where Martha and I were born, now he wanted to be near Jerusalem so we moved to Bethany, he said it was the best thing to do.

When we got there, life was quiet, the house was beautiful and everything was fine, but inside me there was a restlessness to live with the magic that I had known to be, the quiet routine of normal life suffocated me, even as a child. I was a restless child. It was as if I was full of electricity inside me and I needed to spend it in life.

Jesus and his parents lived in En-Nazir, it is not that far, but they didn't travel much, neither did we, so Jesus became like a dream, a beautiful dream of magic and life that wasn't so real. . . Yet, I had already experienced that dream being real in my life. Maybe it was that memory which made me restless and didn't allow me to be just normal like other children were.

On the road that goes from Jericho, going north after you leave Jerusalem, near the river Jordan, there is a little forest and some caves up on the rocks. This area is well known to travelers as a lion's habitat, so they do not get near the caves.

They said that when Jesus passed by the lions started roaring. In one of these caves there was a lioness with four cubs. At once, in front of everyone and without giving his parents the time to react, Jesus walked straight to the caves. Everyone was terrified. He marched into the cave and the cubs, when they saw him, came to play with Him, jumping and nibbling at Him and rolling and turning on the floor in cute postures like kitty cats do. Outside the cave, at certain distance, there were a couple of lions. These didn't move, but were saying hello to Jesus with their tails.

Jesus came out of the cave and the lioness and its cubs followed Him and started playing with Him as if they were kitty cats. Some children wanted to join Him, but He told them not to, for that would be dangerous for them because they are not divine yet and have forgotten how to do what Jesus does, just as it happened to us with the sunray. Seeing this, many of the people took their children with them and ran away. I wish I had been there! The people that were observing all this from afar were horrified. Some thought, *'If this boy, or his parents, was not a great sinner, he wouldn't have walked so spontaneously to the lions.'* Jesus read their thoughts and in a high voice, so that everyone could hear Him, shouted

'How much better are these animals than many of you! How naturally they acknowledge and glorify their Lord!'

Then Jesus bid good bye to the beasts and joined what was left of the group. My father commented that Jesus and his family had moved to Caphernaum near the Sea of Galilee because Joseph gets a lot of work in that city. I wished we would move there. . . But my father has a nice house in Bethany, which is near Jerusalem and that is good for his business. . . I love the Sea of Galilee; I feel that I belong there. Maybe I will move there some day. . .

My brother Lazarus went to stay with them for a month because he's only one year younger than Jesus, so they play together and when he came back he was different. He looked so luminous, so happy and he did so well in school. I wish I could go to visit Jesus, I know it would do me some good, but father said that there were only boys at their home and that only Lazarus could go.

Once in a while we would hear about Jesus, He seemed to have become even more controversial than before. We heard that some of the Rabbis who taught Him were amazed at his wisdom and loved Him, while others were threatened by His knowledge and upset with Him because of it. It seemed to be that wherever Jesus went, He had the virtue of arousing either the best, or the worst in those who were in contact with Him. He was now old enough to go to school and in Palestine there was no child, no matter how young or in what village he lived who was not taught to read, write and to understand the Torah. In the year 103 before Jesus was born, Aristobulus first king of the Jews, (Maccabees) forced all the *'Gentiles'* living in Galilee to adopt circumcision and the Mosaic Law. By this we must understand that after the edict of Aristobulus, all the Gentiles living in Galilee, which included my parents and the parents of Jesus, were Aryans by blood, Gentiles by natural religious classification, mystics by philosophy and Jews by forced adoption.

So, for more than a century all the Gentiles were forced to adopt circumcision, respect the Mosaic Law, and in accordance with this edict all children had to learn the

Torah and accept the Jewish faith at a certain age. Galilee was considered *'the land of the Gentiles.'* This is why I loved Galilee, because the people in Galilee were akin to the mystical teachings of Life, and not to the hard rule of the letter without spirit. It is in Galilee, where most of the teachings of Jesus happened. And it is from Galilee where most of His apostles came from. Galilee was also referred as the land of Hamath, or of the *'hot springs.'* The *'door of Hamath'* is near Magdala where I was born, about three miles north of Tiberiades. I give all these facts so that those who want to know Jesus more in depth can understand many of the seeming contradictions around Him and the things that He had to contend with since the moment that He was born. It will also help some to understand why the Essenes accepted Jesus immediately as their Saviour and the Jews opposed Him so violently instead of accepting Him as the world Messiah, whom they still expect.

Knowing that the parents of Jesus were Gentiles and Essenes will also explain things about the education of Jesus, which if you don't know this, you can't understand. For instance, He stunned all the doctors of the law in the Jewish Temple, who knew they had not taught Him all that He knew and that His wisdom was divine. And when they asked Him who were His teachers, Jesus told them that they were the Essene Magi who tutored and cared for Him throughout all His life and served Him in all that He was going to need for His mission on this earth.

But even if Jesus' grandparents were not Jews, they were obliged as all the Essenes that lived in Judea were, to practice all the Jewish rites. That is the reason why many thought they were Jews. Jesus' grandparents as well as His parents were Aryans, and practicing Essenes. Joachim, the grandfather of Jesus and the older brother of Joseph of Arimathea, was a High Priest in the Holy Temple of Heliopolis in Egypt. In this temple the Essene brotherhood assembled for their high ceremonies, and also they did so for lesser rites in the smaller temple of Helios, called *'Temple of the Sun'* located at the outer gates of Jerusalem.

An angel told Joachim and Anna being well past the age of fertility that Anna would give birth to a child who wasn't the product of sexual copulation between them. The Baby girl was offered to the temple as soon as she was born, she was divinely ordained since her birth and when she was six months old became a *'Dove'* or *'Vestal'* of the Temple. She was given the name of Mary, which means *'Giver of light'* and *'Bitter Sea.'*

When Mary's first birthday came there was a big celebration in the Temple of the Sun, all the Vestals, Priests and Magi of the Temples of the Essene Brotherhood were present and Joachim brought the baby Mary to the sanctuary where she was sprinkled with undefiled rose water and rose petals, and the High Priest prayed saying,

'God has magnified His purpose and His Name in all generations and through this Child, God will manifest His divine Word and redemption to the children of light.'

And the Magi bowed in front of the Baby. And they proclaimed her *'the Dove of the Temple of the Sun.'* Afterwards, they blessed her and proclaimed her name Mary to be a name that was to be eternally blessed by man and angels through all generations to come of the Sons of God. And the vestals of the Temple of the Sun came with the sacred lamps burning with joy at the gift of God to the Temple and they sang to her,

'We sing to you this song, Oh Holy Child, a song to God, for in You He has recreated His Glory,
Listen, you Priests and Magis of the Twelve Kingdoms for the Holy Dove is with us and God abides with us.'

And from out of the space above the altar, archangel Gabriel appeared and gave Mary who floated towards him a morsel of food and the angel said to the Baby,

'Take it, this is to be your food from here on, for you no longer will eat of your mother's food, for you now will eat only from that which your own kind will serve you.'

And since that day, while Mary was in the Temple the angels fed her.

When she was twelve and eleven months old, the Magi came and ask Joachim what they should do because at this age the girls got married and went out of the Temple, but Mary was to be the vessel for God's manifestation so she should be given in marriage to someone who could be trusted to guard her purity. And an angel came to Joachim and told him to summon 144 widowers of the Brotherhood and to have them bring a staff, and that Mary should be given to be cared for to him to whom God would give the sign of His choice.

And there was Joseph, one who was a very devout Essene and when all the widowers were summoned he went to the Temple, not knowing for what reason he was being called. There were 144 sacred staffs, which had been purified, and the High Priest gave one to each of the widowers, but the sign had not been given yet. Joseph was the last to receive one, and as he bowed in front of the High Priest to receive it a white dove hovered over his head and three perfect white lilies sprang out of the staff as a symbol of purity. The High Priest recognizing in Joseph the keeper of Mary's virginal purity said to him,

'Joseph, you have been allowed to receive the 'Dove of the Sun' to guard her in your home.'

Joseph refused arguing that he had already two sons and that he was old and he would be made fun of, having a twelve year old girl as his wife in his home. But the High Priest admonished Joseph, reminding him that it was the will of God, so, Joseph went beyond himself and his fears and offered himself to keep and guard the purity of the sacred vessel of God, the *'Dove of Helios.'*

And this is how the twelve-year-old Mary came to marry Joseph the widower and builder, as the *'Virgin of the Essene Brotherhood.'*

The Temple needed new curtains and the High Priests called seven virgins to cast lots among them to see who should spin the gold for the curtain, and who should spin the fine linen and silk and who should spin the green, the scarlet, the purple and the blue. And the true purple and the scarlet fell to the lot of Mary, and the High Priests knew that those colors were the sign of redemption and of the highest purification and a sign that soon she would give birth to the Saviour they waited for. And when she was starting to spin there appeared to her archangel Gabriel. The archangel in charge of generation knelt in front of her and bowed to her saying, *'Hail Mary, full of Grace, You have found favor in God, may your name be always honored and regarded with devotion, You are blessed among all women, for you shall conceive The Word of God in you Virgin's womb.'*

Mary disputed this asking the angel, *'How can I conceive the Word of God and bear a child in my womb as other women do when I know no man, neither will I ever know one, for I have pledged my virginity to God.'*

And the Archangel answered to Mary, *'You will not conceive in the manner that other women do, but you will bear a child, the Word of God, as others do. The Word of God shall breathe upon You and the Holy Life which shall be born of You shall be called Jesus, the Son of Man and will be God in Man and with Man.'*

At this moment, Mary, this amazing twelve-year-old child, made the greatest decision, which has ever been made on this earth, second only to the one of the Christ to become a Man and die for us. For with her *'yes'* she became the co-redemptor of humanity. Once that it was clear for her that this was going to be God's child and that her purity would not be violated by any man, she said,

'Let it be in me according to the will of the Word of God, for I am His humble servant.'

When Mary took back to the Temple the scarlet and true purple, which she had wrought, the High Priest blessed her and again repeated to her that her name would be holy in all the generations of the earth. *('Mystical Life of Jesus' H. Spencer Lewis)* Most people know the rest of the story in a more or less accurate way. What is not well known, is that Jesus as well as his parents belonged to the Essene sect, and were looked at as *'Gentriles'* opposed to the Jewish doctrines and practices by the Jews. The Essenes were not Jews by birth, blood or by religion. It is natural then that they would establish their communities as far as possible from those who were not agreeable to their presence.

As I said before, the grandparents and parents of Jesus were practicing Essenes, and through their veins flowed Aryan blood. They settled in Galilee, like my parents. At that time, the term Galilean meant *'Gentile'* to the Jews. These things have been confused with the passing of time in such a way that most people think that the family of Jesus was Jewish. Not only was He born into the family of devout Essenes, He was raised in a community of Essenes and educated by Essenes and all that He taught and did was derived from the Essene teachings. He Himself, the Word of God, being the Essence of the Essene teachings and His coming to earth the culmination of them. (Matt. 4, 15. *'Galilee of the Gentiles'*)

How can anyone reconcile the diametrically opposite Jehovian teachings with those of Jesus? They cannot mix because they are as opposite as night and day are. Why do people think that the Jews called Jesus *'the Galilean?'** Maybe people think that Jesus was a Jew because He was circumcised, or because He went to the synagogue?

* **Note.** Galilean meant to the Pharisees and the Sadducees *'someone heathen, a heretic.'*

Jesus was a Jew in the true sense of the word, for He was One with God, but not in the sense of having Hebrew blood. Neither did He approve of the Jehovian rites. The Nazarenes and the Essenes were people of non-Jewish ways and they both had many

57

characteristics in common. It is no secret that the learned Jews called both the Nazarenes and the Essenes *'heretics?'* Are people aware that Jesus did not observe the *'Sabbath?'* Are they aware that He did not approve of blood sacrifices?

In the Jewish tradition women are supposed to not even have a soul and are not worthy of even being spoken to. Jesus not only gave women a special place since the very beginning of his public mission but He made disciples out of us, and let us participate in everything He did.

How can anyone explain all these contradictions without knowing His background? Of all the disciples of Jesus, only three were Jews, Judas, and Paul of Tarsus and Matthew. The rest of us were Galileans. I was openly rebellious to the imposed Jewish traditions on us, others were more subtle, but of Jewish blood most of us were not. Who can think that all of this is just a coincidence?*

* Mary, Joseph and Jesus, along with many others were considered Nazarites, people of a non-Jewish sect. Taking this into consideration we have at once an interesting picture of the conditions existing in and around Palestine just prior to the Christian era. We have, first of all, a large number of men and women, even children, who were either Jewish by birth, Gentile by birth, for of various races and bloods, but who had refused to adopt wholly or completely the Mosaic law, and were Jewish only because the laws of the land forced them to adopt circumcision, to appear in the synagogue when twelve years of age, to study the Torah and to be enrolled as Jews. Yet these persons were mystically inclined in their beliefs, and followed the Jewish teachings only so far as they revealed God and God's laws and served them in their study of the Divine Principles. On the other hand there was a definite organization of mystics known as the Essenes, which conducted many forms of humanitarian activities. They were located in the northern center in Galilee, among the Aryans, because they had been directed to this locality by the center of their organization in Egypt. (*'The Mystical Life of Jesus'* H. Spencer Lewis p.68 69)

Knowing these facts will help anyone to understand better what Jesus had to go through as He grew up and was sent to school. It wasn't easy for Him, being that *'He was Himself 'That' which is the Living Essence of All there is'* therefore, He had by Nature a subjective Knowledge of the Truth and to go to school where He was being forced *'to learn as true,'* that which covered Its magnificence. And learn from those who had no true knowledge of what they were teaching, for they were blinded by sensory limits. What happened in this incident in a school at En-Nazir exemplifies what was an everyday experience for the God Child. There was a teacher at that school, a man called Zaqueo who had heard about Jesus and wanted to know what the child knew.

Joseph, privy to the divine wisdom of Jesus and knowing also that the chief instructors of the Essene community were tutoring him, was reluctant to send Jesus to a normal school. Any Essene child was guaranteed to have the highest education available, but The Essene Masters were providing Jesus with an excellent education, not only as the Son of Man, but also as the Son of God. They taught to Him other things, things of a higher nature, which were necessary to carry out His great mission in life. Zaqueo did not understand why Joseph was reluctant to send Jesus to school, when other children, younger than Jesus had started to attend the class. So, Zaqueo scolded Joseph and said to him,

'What is wrong with you Joseph that you don't send your son to school to instruct him in letter and good ways? Are you placing your son above the tradition of the elders?'

Joseph answered saying that he had the impression that Jesus knew everything. But Zaqueo insisted that this was arrogance on his part and that he should send Jesus to school, so Joseph had no option but to send Him. The God Child came to class, sat quietly and listened attentively to Zaqueo who started explaining the basic things about letters. Zaqueo began with the Greek letters because in Palestine it was necessary to know this language, as the neighbors of Decapolis and Syria would talk in this language for commerce, theater and religious documents, then after he would teach the Hebrew alphabet. So he started drawing with great care and clarity, from the *'Alfa'* to the *'Omega.'*

Jesus then scolded Zaqueo and said, **'How dare you explain to these children the letter 'Beta' when you ignore in your own self the nature of 'Alfa'? Hypocrite! Find first the deep meaning, the true sense of 'Alfa' and explain it! Only then we will believe what you have to say about the other letters.'** (Irineo, *'Adversus Haerese'* 1. 14, 3)

Then the Child questioned Zaqueo about the nature of the first letter, **'Tell me,'** He said, **'Why does it have the line that traverses it? What sense does its homogeneity, equilibrium and proportion have?'**

Zaqueo didn't know what to say, so he asked the child to explain it himself if He knew,

And Jesus said to him, **'Alfa' is the head, the origin of all. And you must know that all the letters have a meaning in themselves, but they all are part of the body of Truth.'**

Zaqueo marveled at His wisdom and when he brought Jesus back to Joseph said,

'Poor me! I do not know what to do now, because I myself have created a royal confusion in the school when I brought your child.

I can't take the severity that I see in his eyes and I do not comprehend his discourse. I thought that I was going to teach him and I have found in him a teacher that I do not know how to follow.

Send him to Levi, in the next town because he is more knowledgeable than I am and he may be able to handle him. Because if no one does, how is he going to learn what he has to?' (Meaning the Jewish teachings) (Gospel of Pseudo Mateo, 6-7)

Joseph was not convinced to send Jesus to Levi, but on the other hand he was put under pressure, because that was the law, and he didn't want the problems that could ensue if he didn't send Jesus to school. Not having any other alternative, the next day Joseph took the God Child to school again.

When Jesus came into the classroom he didn't sit with the other children but alone, in the back of the room.

Levi started his lesson with the letters to see if the Child would speak to him as He had spoken to Zaqueo and often he would pause to ask a question to Jesus, but he didn't get any response from the Child.

Levi had been told that the Child was different and all knowing so he decided to have patience and continue with his lesson.

After a while he asked Jesus, *'Tell me this letter.'*

And again, Jesus didn't respond.

Then Levi lost his temper and taking a stick in his hand walked menacing to where the child was sitting and hit Him on the head with it.

As Jesus felt the pain, He turned to look at the teacher with anger and at that point Levi fainted.

Levi wasn't dead, but he lost his consciousness, so they took him to his home, where he was unconscious for few days. Jesus told Joseph what had happened, and this grieved the old man because of the problems that they had before, so he wouldn't let Jesus out for a while.   *(Gospel of Pseudo Thomas, 14)*

After few days passed, Hillel, who was a High Priest and president of the Sanhedrim, the greatest master among the Jews, came to visit Joseph. He was a wise man and people respected him. He was also a good friend of Joseph of Arimathea, the uncle of Mary, the mother of Jesus. Hillel was intrigued with the Child's knowledge and being one of the Sages who supervised His education, he wanted to hear the God Child's version of the story and see how was He using His power. Secretly, Hillel who held an important position in the Sanhedrim, was also a member of the Essene brotherhood of Sages that had a center on the three Mounts, where Jesus studied. *(Heliopolis,)* But because of his high office among the Jews, Hillel, as well as Joseph of Arimathea and Nicodemus, who also held high offices in the Sanhedrim, was compelled to keep it secret. Yet, some of his famous sayings are based on the principles of the Essene Brotherhood, and parallel to those of Jesus, as, **'Do not do unto others, what is hateful to you.'** While Hillel talked with Joseph he put on the table a book with some comments about the Law that he had brought with him. Jesus saw it and without stopping to read the letters drawn on it started to explain the contents of the book to those in the house. They were all in awe in front of His wisdom. Hillel said to Joseph, *'This child is full of Grace and Divine Wisdom!'*

Jesus heard his words, and turning towards Hillel, said, **'Thanks to you, because you have spoken with righteousness and given testimony to Truth, your colleague who was punished will be healed. Because I know that you came to ask for Grace for him.'**

They say that at the moment He said these words - and this is how the people who saw it told it - Levi came back to consciousness. And Hillel was grateful, for in his heart he had wanted to ask the God Child to bring Levi back to consciousness. But he didn't say anything for he knew that Jesus had apparently become a child highly dangerous to some and feared by them, and Joseph and Mary were concerned for his life. (*'Book of the Infancy of the Savior'* Ms. lat. 11867 Paris, 1. De Santos 221)

Rabbi Barachia of the synagogue of En-Nazir, who helped Mary to teach her son, loved to teach and learn from Jesus. One morning, they say that Rabbi Barachia asked the child, *'Which is the greatest of the Ten Commandments?'*

And Jesus said, **'None is greatest. These are pearls of a necklace and the string that binds them is Love. If one thinks with Love, feels Love, and acts with Love, one will fulfill all other commandments. Love is all we need, for God is Love.'**

Rabbi Barachia was amazed at his answer and asked Jesus who had taught him this truth,

And Jesus answered, *'No teacher. This truth teaches by Itself. If anyone is open they will know for this truth is constant and it's everywhere.'*

Tell me Rabboni, Rabbi Barachia said, *'Whose hand can open a man's mind to let truth enter?'*

And Jesus said, *'It is Love, for God is Love and if a heart is open to Him no matter from what race that man is, God himself will teach that man, in the silent chambers of the heart.'*

When Rabbi Barachia left, Jesus said to Mary that he felt that the Rabbi seemed to think that God favored the Jews above all other men and that this mistake was like a wall built around them, that would cost them much pain. Jesus then said that soon He wanted to go away from Jewry and meet other men, that it was part of His job.

At the time, Archangel Gabriel appeared to Joseph and told him that for the moment he guarded Jesus from His power to know how to read and write, because for a while He was not going to acquire knowledge from books, but from the rapport with the people, the poor, the ignorant and the outcast, for they needed Him most.

The stories and the teachings in them were always wonderful, but I didn't feel the same, something had changed inside me, now the stories about Jesus made me restless, it was as if someone would say to me, *'The Sun is shining in some other place in the earth, but you can't see its light, nor feel its warmth. . . So let me tell you about the Sun. . .'* When I heard these stories, I felt as if it wasn't enough to hear. . . I wanted to feel the warmth of the Sun more and more.

So, the stories would not just enchant me, as when I was a child, but they would fill me up with a very intense impulse to go somewhere, and find that warmth and experience it - but I couldn't just sit there and be satisfied with listening anymore. My sister Martha seemed to be very different, we loved each other, but we didn't understand each other at all, so I kept my restlessness to myself. Lazarus, my brother was not in the same predicate. He would travel to En-Nazir and spend time with them; sometimes he would go and visit for a week and that created problems inside me. I was jealous, I resented all boys, and I resented Lazarus because I couldn't go, although I loved him so much. One couldn't help but to love Lazarus. Everyone loved Lazarus. Jesus did too.

When he came back from En-Nazir, he told us that Jesus was distressed about the conditions of life among the people of En-Nazir, of filth, lack, suffering and unkindness, so far removed from those of peace and plenty he had experienced in Egypt. He accompanied his father to his carpentry workshop, where he would entertain himself doing little projects. There were two incidents that happened while Lazarus was there, in which Jesus helped to correct some errors that Joseph had made in two pieces that had been commissioned to him. In one of the cases it was a very expensive bed, made of exotic cedar, which had been commissioned specially by some Syrian merchants.

The bed was for a rich, young man who was getting married. When the bed was finished, and all the materials had been used, Joseph noticed with dismay that one of the supporting pieces of the infrastructure was smaller than the other. Joseph didn't know what to do, because he couldn't make the bed smaller and he didn't have more wood. When Jesus saw him worrying, he made a simple gesture with his head and made the two pieces be of the same size. (*'Gospel of Pseudo Matheo'* 41)

Something similar happened with a throne, a very special commission of a very rich person of Jerusalem, who had commissioned Joseph to do this work, even if he didn't live near him because he was sure he would do a good job. When Joseph finished the complicated piece, which took almost two years, the measurements were not exact. Jesus told him to pull from one side of the throne, while he pulled from the other. In one moment, the huge throne acquired the desired proportions! (*'Arab Gospel from Jesus' Infancy'* 39)

Lazarus also told us that while he was at their home, Jesus had saved Santiago's life. Maria had sent Santiago to pick some cabbages in a nearby vegetable garden to cook dinner and Jesus insisted in going with him. While Santiago was looking at the cabbages trying to pick the best, a snake, which was hiding under one of them, bit Santiago on his hand. Santiago cried in pain as he felt as if his whole hand was on fire. He was feeling faint and screamed to Jesus not to get near because there was a snake around, to go and get help because it had bitten him. But Jesus instead, came running and when He saw what had happened, called the snake with a strong shout and it immediately appeared instantly in front of Him.

Then Jesus ordered the snake, **'Suck all the poison back into yourself that you have injected in my brother!'**

The snake came crawling to Santiago and sucked all the poison back, after which the child told it that it deserved its own poison, and the snake exploded. Then Jesus breathed on Santiago's hand, and in an instant it was as if nothing had happened to it. (*'Gospel of Pseudo Mateo'* 41: *'Arab Gospel of the Infancy of the Savior'* 42)

When I heard these stories, I said to myself, *'I wish He could take the poison I have inside me about Lazarus being able to go and visit Him,'* but I just keep those thoughts to myself. Nobody knows. I know that if I would say it, no one could understand me. I don't really know if I understand myself. It has to do, I think with being told all the time that woman are defiled, and that they are not the same, and then this thing of Lazarus being able to go and visit Jesus to top it all. I know I have to keep it

all to myself, but it eats me up. The other day I pushed Lazarus and he fell. I felt awful after I did it, but before I pushed him I really wanted to make him fall!   Lazarus also saw Jesus save the life of a young boy, who had cut his hand off himself with an ax while cutting wood, and was bleeding to death. He said that when was lying in the floor bleeding to death Jesus happened to pass by, so He came to the boy and told him in the most natural way, *'Get up, continue cutting wood and remember me from now on when you do.'*

And when He said these words the hand and the arm put themselves together as if nothing had happened. He also brought back a child from the dead and healed other children of different illnesses. (*'Gospel of Pseudo Thomas'* 17 and *'Arab Gospel of the Infancy of the Savior'* 27, 28, 30)

There were many incidents like these, as I said before it is impossible for me, or anyone else to tell all the wonders and miracles and all the outpouring of love and wisdom and fun and magic with which His whole life was full of, so one needs to be very discriminative when one talks about His life. I will tell you those things, which had a stronger impact in my life. This doesn't mean that those were the greatest miracles He did, but just that those are the incidents that I either had the luck to experience personally, or that I was told about and affected mine. One of these occasions was His seven years old birthday party. Jesus is going to be seven years old and we have been invited to his grandparent's house, Joachim and Anna, to celebrate it, they live in Jerusalem. He said that when grandfather Joachim, told Jesus that he would give Him whatever He desired for His birthday, Jesus answered that what He wanted was their permission to go out and invite children who were in need and give them clothing and toys and celebrate His birthday with them. Joachim and Anna were pleased and allowed Jesus to do so, the fact that they live in simplicity, my father, explained, is a choice not a necessity.

Joachim, as well as his brother Joseph of Marmore and of Arimathea, is enormously rich. He gives a third of his income to the poor, a third to the Synagogue and he lives with what is left. He is a very generous man and he is very pleased with the choice Jesus has made.

We have also been invited! My father says that it is good for us to experience the *'joy of giving'* especially me, because I have asked for too many presents for my birthday which is coming soon. This is because I start asking for my birthday presents like six months before it comes, just to remind my father that it's coming and of what I want to get. Martha is better, she is more content with what she gets, and Lazarus gets what I tell him to ask for, he is easy to convince and he likes it, because that way we can enjoy his toys together. We all can't wait to go to the party. I feel happy and nervous, I don't know why. What is He going to do? His grandparent's house was full of children, there were about a hundred children there, and Jesus served everyone personally. There was food and toys for everyone, but He didn't spend special time with anyone. It seemed as if He was there for all and for none. . . I wanted special attention from Him, so I felt a little disappointed, although I had a lot of fun and was more than happy to be there too.

His mother was telling my father about an incident that happened with Jesus and a water jug. She said that one day she gave Jesus a clay jug so that he would bring water from the fountain. Jesus went, but on the way back, he bumped with another child and the jug broke. Jesus came back to the fountain feeling pretty discouraged because he didn't want to come back home without the water she needed. But, once at the fountain, he had the idea of extending the robe that he was wearing and use it as a jug to collect the water, so He filled it up with water and brought home the quantity of water that His mother needed. She said that seeing this wonder she kissed Him, and kept in her heart one more mystery of the many that she had witnessed, and that she couldn't tell anyone. (*'Gospel of Pseudo Mateo'* 11)

It seemed as if even the elements became different when He was there, they just became what He wanted them to be with no effort or spells, just with his wish.   I smiled at Him when she finished the story and He smiled back at me. I will always remember this day! To hear this story made me happy because it reminded me of that day in which He walked on the sunray! Since that day, whenever I see the sunrays breaking through my window, I think of Him, it seems to me that the light and I are smiling with each other, because we both know a secret. . .   Those things make my heart happy.

From now on I will also think of Him when I go to the fountain. Why do I think of Jesus so much? He doesn't seem to pay any special attention to anyone. . . Anyone means me. That upsets me. I wish that He had a birthday everyday, or that we could travel to where they live, then we would become friends. I am sure of that because He smiled back at me as if we both know a secret. . . I know what my secret is, but what is His secret I wonder. . ?

Few years had passed; it has been a long time. . . I'm ten years old but I look thirteen. Nobody knows my real age just by looking at me. People say that I'm beautiful. They comment on my beauty pretty often. I look at myself and I don't know what it is to be beautiful. They say my eyes are big, my eyelashes long and my lips are sensual and red like the pomegranate and that my walk reminds them of a cat. I like the comparisons, I look at myself in an Egyptian mirror which once belonged to my mother and wonder. . . How do others see me? What is to be beautiful?

 I love to dance and be free.   There are flowers in my garden who look like angel's trumpets, and have a perfume which intoxicates - a friend told me to eat some seeds if I wanted to have a wonderful experience. . . He said sometimes you die if you eat them, sometimes you go places where your body can't take you to, so I did try them and I didn't die, these seeds made me see and think beautiful things. . .   I don't think I'll tell anyone about this, I'll just share these experiences with my friend. Maybe my parents would not like it but I do, although these experiences are disappointing in a way, because you see beautiful things but the experience doesn't last long, so you are back where you started.   It's like going to Egypt and coming back; it's not the same as when we lived there. I want more. . .

The bedtime stories gradually stopped, I guess it is just part of growing up, because as good as they were, bedtime stories about Jesus were not enough for me anymore, they were just like having a glass of water in the middle of the desert at high noon. . . No, the stories were not enough for me. I wanted to experience them.

I didn't like living in Bethany, the Jewish teachings were enforced in this area and they were not appealing to me at all, woman were kept behind a screen because they were not considered worthy to come in where the men were. I hated that! Jehovah was too angry, too scary for me to feel attracted to him. I couldn't envision a God like that; I always felt that God should attract us through love, that man ought to feel magnetized by God as my Essene and Hindu friends from school tell me. They are attracted to their God, whom they call Christ or Krishna and is the Supreme Lover.

The conditions in Palestine are crazy. We are immersed in a mess of beliefs and practices and I get confused. There is not one language spoken, but many languages. Not one interest, but many diverse interests. It is a country of mixed people who are overtly hostile to the ways, or to the beliefs of others. Those of the Jewish denominations are not all Hebrews, the Saducees hate the Pharisees and the Pharisees hate the Samaritans and the Saducees, but they all join in hating us *'Gentiles.'* There are Syrians, Grecian, Phoenicians, Romans, Egyptians and they all contend for mastery. There are Heathen temples and rites, Jewish temples and rites and in the middle of the mess there are the Nomads, wild people living without restraint or regulation, I tend to be attracted to their ways rather than to all these others.

The Essene colony is quiet and nobody knows much about them. We, the Essenes are considered *'heretics'* by the Jews and forced to do all their rites and study their teachings. I am confused, I like to fantasize that I am a Nomad and live in the desert free of all this! But I am here and I don't like it. Everyone seems to think that they are right and are violently opposed to the customs of the others. It is impossible to have peace and harmony amongst these people, they are always fighting and cursing and throwing stones. I hate it.

I wish we would go back to Galilee, but we are now living in Bethany, which is considered a heathen district by the Jews. They consider the land near Antioch the only real and true land of Israel. Who cares! Bethany house is nice, but the mountain is not as beautiful to me as the Sea of Galilee, nor are the people as nice as the people who live in Galilee. To be a Gentile is supposed to be a bad thing, we Galileans and Essenes are looked at as *'Gentiles,'* I like that. I refuse to be educated as a Jewess, and I will not go to the Synagogue unless I feel equal to the men.

I will not go to a place of worship where women are considered defiled and treated like a pest that needs to be kept away from the *'holy'* men. They lust at my sight at every opportunity they get. No! I won't go! My father has begged me to comply and I rebel and throw a tantrum. I won't go; my dislike about this type of treatment to women is stronger than my desire to please my father. I love my father, but this is for me a question of life or death. He does not understand, he thinks that I am just being obstinate, but I will not give up, that's the end of the issue.

My father has tried everything, nothing works. He worries about my rebellious nature, for neither rewards, fear, nor punishment makes me change my mind when its set on something so important to me as this issue is. One day, I know that I will find a God who is true to my heart and my true feelings, not someone imposed on me, as they say, *'The river flows towards the Ocean, no matter who likes it or not.'*

I haven't seen the Ocean yet, but in my heart I know as the Greeks say that if I am true to myself, I cannot go wrong.   I long for Jesus. . .   I wonder often about His feeling about all these things that I rebel against.

I often thought that I was bad because I couldn't accept things so easily as others seemed able to do. . . It was as if I had a glimpse of a wonder which no one can even imagine, and I was forced to live a normal life. . .! I couldn't be normal; I was restless and driven by that restlessness, I felt that it was useless for me to lie to myself.

No, rituals and words were not enough for me.   I wanted an experience, I didn't want people to talk to me about a banquet, I wanted to be part of it and eat and drink and experience the banquet!   So, as I grew up I started trying to find that banquet which everybody talked about. . . Anywhere. . . And everywhere. . . .

Yes, you can say that I Mary was the black sheep of the family. No one knew what I wanted, because I didn't really know what that ardor in me was. . . Or what it really wanted, but I knew what I didn't want to become, or end up doing, just by accepting what others told me I should be, or do. So, I tried to satisfy myself with one thing and the other, I was inventive but not successful in finding satisfaction, and wanted and wanted. . . More and more, but I was never satisfied.

I heard that Jesus was in Jerusalem for the Feast of the Tabernacles, and although my father invited them to stay with us, they didn't, because they are traveling in a caravan with many other people who come from Galilee for the festivities. We were also there, but there were so many people we didn't see them. Jesus and I are now twelve years old, we are only months apart but He seems to do and know things that not even His elders know how to do. I can't understand why He is and He is not like us.

Sometimes I see Jesus as one of the Gods from the Greek Myths, that's why I would like to be near Him always, because life is special if one is near Him. It seems that one is in the Olympus and that everything, even the rocks become alive.

Because I cannot travel where Jesus is, I see Him in my mind and talk to Him a lot, and when I am afraid at night when I wake up in the dark I ask Him to come and put some light around me and I dream beautiful dreams of wonder lands where everything is perfect and we play with the stars. . . I wait day and night for the day when He will be back, and He will make our life luminous and magic again. . . Meanwhile I play with my brother and sister, who also love Him, but not as much as I do, a game in which we bet to win who will be the one of us who hears news about Him first, and we constantly accost our father asking him for Jesus' whereabouts. I pray every night that he comes back before I become really old like my father and can't play with Him anymore. . .

Once in a while we hear from Jesus, because all the Essene community follows his steps and observes Him closely. My father's friends often tell us stories about Him. I heard that His people had come as they do every year, for the Feast of the Passover and that when they were on the way back, Joseph and his mother could not find Jesus amongst the children of their party. No one could find Him, so they returned again to Jerusalem looking for Him and after three days of great anxiety, they found Him in the temple sitting in the midst of the priests and doctors of the Law, who were astonished at His knowledge.

Among the things they commented that Jesus asked was, *'Who is the Messiah a descendant of?'*

And they answered, *'Of King David'*

Then they said that Jesus told them, *'Why then is it that David calls Him His Lord when he says of him, 'God said to my Lord, sit to my right until I put your adversaries at your feet.'* (*'CF .Mt'*. 22, 42, 46)

Then one of the priests asked Him if He had read books and learned this from the books He read.

And Jesus responded, *'Yes, I read and I assimilate all that they contain in essence.'*

And immediately started to explain to them the mysteries of Genesis, the prophets' insight and things that the human mind is slow to comprehend.

And the priest said, *'I must confess that until today I have never had the opportunity to learn or hear such profound meaning to these things. Who do you think this child is?'*

Then Jesus inquired of the priests the cause of so much suffering and want and unkindness when there was plenty for all. And asked them why was it that one who expressed a criticism would have his head cut off? One of the priests asked Him where He had been to get such ideas,

And Jesus replied, *'In the three mountains near the Nile.'*

There was one of them who was an astronomer and asked Jesus if He knew anything about this science.

And Jesus told him of the number of celestial spheres and bodies that are in the firmament, he explained to him their nature and properties, and about their retrograde positions, of their triad, square, and hexagonal aspects, of their comings and goings, and their positions and many other things that this man didn't know.

And there was a physician and He asked Jesus if He knew anything about the human body.

And Jesus explained to him the physical, metaphysical, hyper physical and hipo physical forces of the body, its energies and the effects of heat and dryness, of cold and humidity and the results of all these things.   And He explained to him the role of the soul in the body, its sense and its effects; and in what consists the faculties of speech, of rage, of desire, to articulate and what is confusion and chaos and disease.   And the doctor did not have the capacity to understand it all.

At this the philosopher bowed in front of Jesus and said, *'My Lord, from now on I will be your disciple and your servant.'*

And they didn't know how He had been able to master as a child, what others require a lifetime of study and devotion to learn, for He knew everything about physics, astronomy, theology and everything else, which not even those who are considered illumined knew.

They said that He was pretty happy conversing with the doctors and that He wanted to stay in the temple but Mary took Him home. We both are now twelve years old, I am few months older and I don't know these things.   Where does He know all that from? I know my father says that He is the Messiah, but what is the Messiah? He is still a child like all other children, I feel that someone has had to teach Him all that, if not how does He know? The truth is that I am always confused about Jesus. I am smart, but I don't know those things, neither do any of my friends, or anyone I know. Then, when we used to know Him, He was always so normal and unassuming, like if He was just one of us. . . He is a mystery to me. . . He is a mystery even to His parents; they were astonished when they found Him teaching things that they never heard of, to the doctors of the Law. Mary then, said to Him, *My son, why have you done so to us? We have been looking for you with much anxiety.'*

And Jesus answered her, *'Did you not know that I would be in the house of my Father? I must take care of my Father's business.'*

They couldn't understand Him, and neither do I. Sometimes I'm confused about Him too, He looks like all of us, but He's so different. I feel that He is very lonely because there is nobody like Him. Nobody understands what He does, nobody, not even I who love Him so. Not even His mother. I wish I had been there. . . I would like to be closer to him and love Him even if I don't understand, so that He doesn't feel so alone. It most be lonely to be so different. I know, because it is lonely for me to not be able to be understood, not even by the people who love me, even though what I keep to myself is nothing special. The people who were in the temple say that He's so unassuming and natural that He makes it seem as if His knowledge is normal, because He speaks in such a way that everyone understands. But the Rabbis, who are supposed to know about these things say that there was no question, no matter how deep it was, that He couldn't answer with unheard of wisdom, sometimes even beyond their own understanding. They said they felt that His knowledge is divine and not of this world, and everyone was amazed.

He's now like a dream to me, like a legend that is near and yet so far. . . It's almost as if I had invented Him to have magic in my life, yet I know He's real, so I want to see Him. I don't even know what He looks like now. My friend Shulaskma was going to Nazareth and she knows how to draw portraits of people very fast and accurately, so I asked her to draw a picture of Jesus and in exchange I would give her my moon stone bracelet that she likes so much.

I waited anxiously for Shulaskma's return because I wanted to know very badly what He looks like now. Very badly, I have certainly changed and I wonder how He has changed. . . But Shulaskma came back with nothing! I was so disappointed! She said that she went to a place where young people gather to talk and play and she saw Him talking to a group of them and she got so immersed in Jesus and what He was saying, that she forgot everything! I still gave her the bracelet though, because she meant to do it.

She described Him to me as well as she could.   So, all I have is a picture in my mind of Him looking at me when I last saw Him years ago. . .   I can see every detail so clearly in my mind. . . He was holding Mary's hand and was wearing a straw hat, which Lazarus used to wear, and gave Him as a souvenir. Suddenly He turned His head and looked at me with an expression, which I can't well describe. . . . But when Jesus looked at me He looked very sad. . .   And it was as if He knew that it was the last time that He was seeing me. . . I felt that He was saying to me a deeper good-bye than just a good-bye.

It was as if He knew that it was the last time that He was seeing me.

I myself must say good bye to you now for the reason that I told you in the first page, that if I would write all the stories about Jesus that I know I am afraid that I would never stop writing, this book would never see an end and. . . It would never get to you. Before I go, I must stress one thing good for you to remember: This book is a book of Love, about the life of Love Himself, who left His magnificent Kingdom of Heaven where everything is perfect to come to visit us on earth as Jesus, just to teach us how to Love. He did that because He loves us and He wants us to be with Him forever in His perfect Kingdom of Life. So, it is good to learn what He taught.

I hope that reading these stories about Baby Jesus will help you to become a lover of His, as I am, for He makes your life shine and your heart happy and He is the best friend that anyone can have. I know that He showers upon you all His Love and His Light everyday, you will only have to open up to receive it and then enjoy it. I have written these stories that I know about Him with all my Love as an offering of gratitude to Jesus for all that He has given to us and for you children to know that you have in Him the best of friends. I hope that you enjoyed them and that you grow up knowing that what He taught us to be is good for us, He said, *'Love each other as I have loved You'* and everything else will be fine. So, if we want to have a happy planet, we must do as Jesus told us to do, for all things like to be loved and everybody is happy if they feel love.

Four Prayers to Say to Baby-Jesus at Night

These are some of the prayers that I said to Jesus, before I went to sleep at night and I was afraid because everything around me was dark and scary, or when I just wanted to feel His love and His Company and see Him in my dreams. They have helped me to feel His Love and His protection throughout my life, I hope that they will do the same for you.

Mary of Bethany

I

May Your Divine Love illumine my life.

And protect me from my bad thoughts,

Bad feelings and from any bad actions

I could take.

In the name of the Father, the Son

And the Holy Ghost. Amen.'

II

'Little Baby-Jesus, light of my life,

You are God but also a little child, just as I am.

This is why I give you lots of love

And all my heart and soul tonight!'

III

'With Baby-Jesus in my heart I go to sleep,

With Baby-Jesus in my mind in the morning I rise,

And at night, the Virgin Mary tucks the two of us in bed

And to protect me from all evil,

Covers my bedroom with her mantle full of stars.'

IV

'Baby Jesus, Baby Jesus

My sweet friend and companion

Please protect me from evil

Be it day or night.'

A Story to Understand

And

A Few Exercises

to

Be Able to See

The

Light of Baby Jesus

That

Shines Inside You

And

Gives You Peace

Illustrated by the author

If you have been told that *you are* a boy named John, Christopher, or any other name. . .

Or a girl named Alexandria, Mary, Cathy, or something like that. . .

If you have been told that
your Daddy, your Mommy and
your teacher *are this* . . .

You have been told that *they are,*
what they seem to be . . .
But that's not *what they really are.*

You have been told that *you are*
what *you seem to be* . . .
But that's not *what you really are.*

If you have been told that
your friends *are this*. . .

You have been told your friends *are,*
what *they seem to be* . . . .
But that's not *what they really are.*

If you have been told that
your house is this. .

You have been told the house is,
what *it seems to be* . . .
But that's not *what it really is.*

If you have been told that
a dog *is this* . . .

and a cat *is this* . . .

You have been told a dog and a cat *are,*
what *they seem to be* . . .
But that's not *what they really are.*

If you have been told that
the sun *is this* . . .

and the moon *is this* . . .

You have been told *they are,*
what *they seem to be.* . .
But that's not *what they really are.*

If you have been told that
a tree *is this* . . .

and an apple *is this* . . .

And flowers *are this* . . .

You have been told *they are,*
what *they seem to be*
But that's not *what they really are.*

7

WHAT ARE THEY THEN?

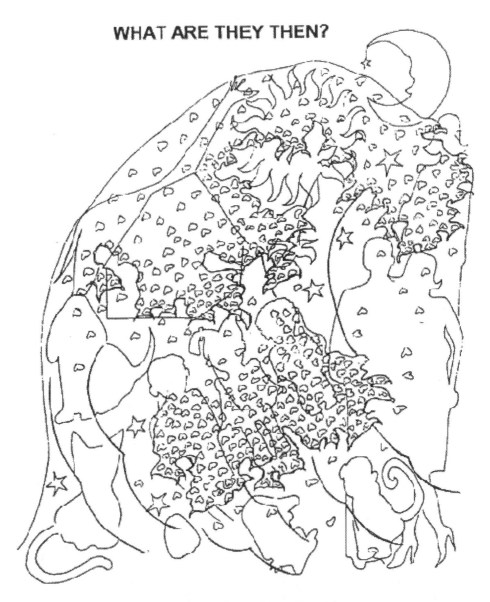

They <u>are</u> all parts of The Breath of Love.
That's what they *really are*.

I could tell you the same about a rabbit, a monkey, a
giraffe, an ice-cream, a mountain, the ocean and the stars . . . I
could go on, and on, and use all the paper that there is in the world,
to tell you - the same thing about *everything* that there is - but then, I
run the risk of forgetting to tell you, the most important thing. So, I'll
just tell you, that all the different forms and shapes you see - people,
animals, mountains, flowers, planets and stars, everyone and
everything you can see, think of, or imagine - *are not what they
seem to be* - what *they truly are* is parts of the Breath of Love, which
you cannot see with your eyes. Nobody can, I'll tell you why:

Everything that you can see, touch, think of, or even the air and things that you cannot see - everything that there is, is LOVE, and Love is Light. Light being the fastest moving thing we know . . .

As a matter of fact - that is what everything is - all matter is light moving slow. It is good to remember that all there is - is light moving slow. And that Light is Love! Everything, even the walls, chairs, stones, and all other things that *look like* if they are stiff are made of Light moving slow.

Some things are moving fast, some slow and some in between. It is the different speed of that movement, which makes some of them be soft or hard, and look like this,

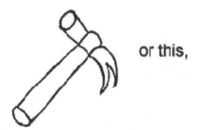

or this,

or this.

If things move very, very fast, we cannot see them with the eyes. The Breath of Love moves very, very fast - so fast it moves that if we were able to see it with our eyes, it would seem to be still.

The Breath of Love moves faster than *pure light,* because Love is where light and everything there is comes from.

This is the reason why you cannot see it with your eyes, touch it with your hands, hear it with your ears, or understand it with your mind.

"If this is so," some people may say, "The Breath of Love is not *real.*" But they are wrong. The Breath of Love *IS* the *only real* thing *there is.*

This is a *very important* secret that I learned some time ago, when I was a small child, from two great friends.

They gave me the most important advice I ever got in my whole life, they said: "What is essential is invisible to the eyes. You only see with the heart." This very simple advice, did two good things for me: 1) It helped me to find The Breath of Love.
 2) It saved me from becoming a grown-up.

I grew bigger, as it is natural, so, I am now what you would call, "a big child", but I never became "grown-up-like."

Why is it so bad to become a grown-up, and important to stay childlike? Because grown-ups have lost the ability to see with the heart - so they can't see The Breath of Love - only children can do that.

So, if you follow the directions as I did, I assure you that you will find The Breath of Love. Once that you are together with IT, you will never feel scared, or sad, or lonely again, because you will feel loved, protected and happy all the time as I do.

Things To Do To See And Feel The Light Of Love

The first thing to do is easy - Feel - feel your breath. Feel and breath very slow. . . Very deep . . . very slow. Breathe in . . . Hold your breath for 4 counts and breathe out . . .   Do that again . . and again . . .

The slow breath will take you to the Breath of Love which is like a Lost Treasure. It is hidden in a magic place inside you. A place full of Light, where Love and Peace dwell, and the heart gets happy.

This is the place your slow breath will help you to find.

The next fun thing to do is to get in touch with the Light.
Not the light of the sun, the moon or the stars, or the electric light,
but a light which is hidden inside you!

As I told you before (page 10) and I hope you remember well - light is the fastest moving thing we know - so, by getting together with the lights we have inside us, we will start to move faster, and faster inside, and get closer, and closer to The Breath of Love. To get in touch with the lights inside you - just read carefully, the directions I will give you and when you finish reading all of them, do everything step by step,. These are the most important instructions that you ever got in your life, so, follow them carefully;

1. Look for a nice, quiet place where you can be alone, and no one, not even your dog, or your kitty-cat can disturb you, sit like this on a pillow, resting your back against the wall, so that you are comfortable. Kitty cats may want to sit in your lap while you do this - mine does - that's fine, they get very quiet and purr because they also like the Breath of Love - they won't bother you.

2. Breath the slow breath. Rest your elbows on your knees and put your thumbs inside your ears, like this, so that there aren't any noises coming from the outside.

3. Keep breathing the slow breath and keep the thumbs inside your ears, close your eyes, and put the little fingers over them, so that they press against the bridge of your nose, like in the drawing.

4. Just sit and enjoy *for a good time*, seeing and hearing all those beautiful lights and wonderful sounds happening inside you.

The lights and music that live in your heart, are good and fun to watch and do, for they will take you closer, and closer to The Breath of Love.

The lights will travel, change shape, color, and form many, many different things - things that I cannot tell you - because each time you see the light, it's different. Each time there is a surprise, and new and unique things happen. Things that no one has ever seen before, and will never be seen again, so, it never gets boring. At the same time that it shines, and does all these nice things, the light dances to the music of thousands of little bells, harps, crickets singing, sounds like the sound of a waterfall, rumbling thunder, and many other beautiful sounds!

All these sounds, lights and Love that you hear, see and feel inside you are natural, because that's what you really are - you are Love that got lost in that which *seems to be*, and light that has gone slow and didn't hear its own music anymore - because *you forgot the way to be One with Love** - but now, you can start to vibrate faster, and faster inside, because you are together with The Breath of Love again!

Everybody has music and light inside them, like you do, because they all are parts of The Breath of Love. *That is what they really are.* The problem is - that if they haven't discovered the lights and the music they make inside - they don't know what they *are*, and consequently they behave like grown-ups and are not happy, because their happiness depends on things that come and go, and change, and sometime go away for good.

Now, let's go to step 5, which is very simple. With your eyes closed and your ears well covered as you already know, keep

listening to all the wonderful sounds and looking at the light on top of your head . . . Stay there quiet . . . wait for a time and . .

something magic will happen . . .   Your breath will start to speak to you!   Listen to what your breath says - each time you inhale, your breath says "I", and each time you exhale, it says "Love", "I . . . . Love. . .   I. . . Love . . .   I. . . Love . . ."   Just be still, and let that silent voice speak to you of Love. . .   Love like you never imagined. Love that will always be there whenever you need Love, or company, or anything else, even when things are crazy, and things go stupid and difficult in the outside, even when you are feeling sad, or guilty, or angry, or bad, or when you are punished and you feel that nobody loves you . . . and you want to cry yourself to sleep. . .

Whenever things go like that, just remember to go inside.. and wait . . ., listen . . ., experience the magic of Love . . .   It will dry your tears, and make all problems disappear. . ., Just Listen and experience. . .   The experience will get stronger, and stronger, and pretty soon you will start to feel good and warm all over, and happy and loved again. . .   then, you will start to realize that Love is always there. . . that you aren't even breathing . . .   It's The Breath of Love who is breathing you!   Yes, IT is constantly breathing you, taking care of you, giving you life and protecting you . IT is saying . . . . I. . . . Love. . . . to you with each breath, even when you are asleep or your are not listening.

The next good and fun thing to do is to breathe in all the Love you can, by just letting yourself go into The Breath of Love with each breath!

This breath can take you to places that you cannot even imagine, much, much better than Disneyland, movies, or any thing you have ever seen or imagined. . .! So, if you want to travel to the Divine Realm of Light inside you, just let yourself go and allow The Breath of Love to take you there. An endless treasure of Love is there, waiting for you to discover it!

Keep listening with your heart to the I. . . . Love. . . . silent voice of your breath. . . feel the Love real strong, so strong that you feel it tingle all over you . . so nice, so sweet . . . so much Love . . .! The Breath of Love, will then wrap you up, and roll you over, and over, taking you to the very depths of the Ocean of Love, where you, and I, and everything came from.

The Breath of Love says I. . . love. . . to you with each breath.

If you do this as much as you can, this Love will get stronger and stronger, and you will feel better and better everyday. And what is better still, is to know that no one can take The Breath of Love away from you.

Now that you have learned to see, hear and be together with The Breath of Love - your eyes are open. You see things in a very, very different way/ You don't see things *only as they seem to be*, but you see all things, even the ones that look stiff, as they *really are*.

Now you know - that all there is, is One Breath of Love - and all that *it seems to be,* belongs to IT.

Now *you know*, the hidden treasure of Love, and also the way to feel it all the time. A very important secret, which will make your life very, very happy,

One good thing to do is - to practice more and more this Love Formula, as much as you can - because the more you do the happier you will be.

In case that you start seeing things as *they seem to be*, and feel separated from Love again

instead of seeing *what they really are*, and *feel One with all there IS.*

Just remind yourself over and over again, that everybody and everything - Daddy, Mommy, teachers, friends, pets, trees, stones, mountains, stars, or flowers - everything and everyone has inside The Breath Who sings I. . . . Love. . . . The reason why this Love Breath is always happy, is because IT Loves the whole Universe, without making differences because someone is small, or nice or tall, or white, or black, or brown, or an animal, plant, stone or star . . so, if we want to feel love and be happy all the time, we should learn to do the same.

You may be wondering, "If everybody has inside the breath that speaks 'I Love' - how come they are not happy?"

It's very simple, the reason why everybody is not happy, especially the grown-ups, is because they have forgotten to feel The Breath inside them Who sings I. . . . Love. . . . In some cases even if you remind them of IT, most of them get to busy with "matters of consequence" and forget It again!   If they only understood that The Breath of Love is all there IS, I'm sure that they would not behave like that - they would open their hearts and feel the Breath of Love. Then, instead of wandering about all stressed out and angry, they would have peace and become happy, like you and me, and they would give lots of Love to everything!

Have you understood what everything and everybody *really is*? If you haven't, no big deal, just take your time and read pages 1 to 10 again. In order to understand well new ideas it is good to repeat them in your mind a few times.

As you know, outside we are all different, some of us are white, red, yellow or black. Some millionaires, some rich and some poor. Some pretty, some not, some tall, some short, some fat, some thin and all that. But inside we are all equal, we all have music, and light and love movements. We are all beautiful and rich inside. Love has no favorites, so Love has given to all of us this beautiful Light which shines all the time, and radiates Love, and the music that gives Peace and makes the heart happy.

That is what we all really are - children of Love
who radiate light, music and love!

HOW TO HELP GROWN-UPS

If you tell this to the grown-ups, maybe some of them will point t
their midriff will say: "Nonsense, this is who I am!"
Poor grownups! They are convinced
they are *what they seem to be*!
But that is not what
they truly are. What
they are is:
Light, Music
and Love Movement!
If they were to insist,
tell them there is
"solid proof" of what
you are saying.
Tell them - in case
they don't remember -
that some time ago,
a very respectable
man of science came
up with a formula
which proves that
all there is - is Light!

Then the grown-ups may ask, (because they think children don't know these thengs) "And who was that? And what did he say?" Tell them that his name was Albert Einstein and the formula that proves what you are saying to be true is E=mc2.

Don't worry about the letters and numbers put together like that - all that it means is: All matter can be turned into Light if its speed is raised to the square of the speed of Light.

Conclusion - "Solid-looking" things are light moving slow; therefore if we speed up their vibration to the square of the speed of light, they can be turned back into light.

I am sorry if I got a little complicated there, grown-ups love complicated statements and take numbers very seriously. We should not hold this against them, but understand their limitations, and try to explain Light and Love to them in their terms, so that they can also learn about The Breath of Love. This is the only reason why I have drawn those blackboards full of numbers and formulas, because I love grown-ups also - so, I excuse myself to you children, in the name of Love.

HAPPINESS FORMULA

So, if you want to be happy and experience Love the rest of your life, you always remember:

1) To go inside to watch the lights, hear the music, and let The Breath of Love wrap you up, and roll you closer, and closer to Love everyday.

2) Remember as much as possible, to see everyone and everything as parts of The Breath of Love.

These two things are good, easy and nice to do. If you do them everyday, you will never feel sad, or scared, or lonely - not even when you go to a new school, or people make funny faces, or call you names - because you *will know* that at all times, The Breath of Love is singing to you "I Love you".

You will always feel free, full of light and love, and all kinds of nice things will start to happen. You will be in love even with those who are angry at you, or upset at themselves, and used to scare you when they were not being nice - because nothing can make you forget The Breath of Love and its magic feeling!

Nobody can do that, you will be happy at all times, even when the things in the outside change, and seem to be upside-down, because things in the outside are never the same - sometimes your best friend is friends with somebody else, sometimes he loves you, sometimes the teacher picks on you and the whole class makes fun of you, sometimes you lose your pet, sometimes you get a new one, and even Daddy and Mommy, sometimes have time to love you and take care of you, and sometimes they don't - but The Breath of Love is always, always with you - loving you, giving you life, saying always "I Love you" with each breath.

At night, when you go to bed, wrap yourself up in The Breath of Love. IT will protect you, make you feel good, and take you to the Realm of Light where you and I and everything else came from. Your dreams will get better, and better and you will be happy to go to sleep.

You will never be afraid of darkness, or dragons and monsters again, or of being left alone, for The Breath of Love is always with you, protecting and loving you, even when you are asleep, and you don't know it.

As soon as you open your eyes in the morning, go inside yourself and say good morning to the lights, the music and The Breath of Love that lives in your heart, you will immediately start to feel good and happy, and free, so good as you never felt before.

Take the Breath of Love to school with you, and you will find that school, and everyplace you go is nice, because the friend who sings "I love" inside you, is there with you.

Tell Daddy and Mommy, your friends and teacher - about the love you feel - It's good to talk to everybody about The Breath of Love, because it will make IT grow more and more.

It is also good to know that not everybody listens the same way, so maybe some of them will see you happy and will want to know the secret you have; some may think that you are lying, some may even make fun of you and others may be to busy to listen about love; don't be disappointed, it is not their fault - we have to have a lot of compassion - especially for grown-ups, because they are to busy being practical, and Love, it's not "real" to them, it's considered non-practical, it can't be touched, not weighed, not banked - so they don't want to invest much time talking about it.

Don't worry, just go inside and feel The Breath of Love, and you will feel happy again. No matter what other's attitude may be - as long as you feel, and see The Breath of Love in everything, everywhere, and everyone - you will be happy and strong all the time.

The more times you listen to The Breath that says "I Love", the closer you will be to Love, and then the music and the lights inside of you will get better and grow brighter, so, pretty soon you will be radiating this Love to the outside, and then . . . many magic things will happen . . .

Your life will become little by little, like a happy song, because as you know, the animals, plants, stones, mountains, flowers and stars are also part of The Breath of Love.

They can feel - when someone knows Love and is together with IT. They will all be nice and speak to you the silent language of Love. The mountains, the stones, the flowers, everything will be saying to you "I Love" . . . "I Love". . .

At night, when you look at the stars, you will be happy, because they are your friends, you know now that inside each one of them, there is a magic voice singing "I Love you." Yes, you will smile with the stars, because you know what they are saying inside.

The animals will also become friends and play with you in a very special way, for they know, that you know the secret of Love .

When people see someone smiling with the stones, and the stars, either they think one is crazy, or they ask the reason why you are doing that. Tell them about The Breath of Love and how you found it. Tell them also, that the most important thing - is to remember The Breath of Love as much as possible, and to see everyone as part of It, no matter what they do. That is the secret of true happiness and perfect Love. Love that always is there for you - no matter how crazy things get around you.

Then, you will have done them the greatest service that you can do for anyone - because if they listened with the heart, they will be interested and try to find The Breath of Love inside them, then they will never have to be grown-ups, or scared, or sad, or lonely again . . .

We want everybody to become happy children, because if more of us are happy, there will be more people in love, and if more people are in Love, more people will want to know The Breath of Love, and if more people know that they are not what they seem to be, but One Breath of Love, Who only knows how to make everybody happy and be in Love, the whole world will shine with light and sing I . . . Love . . ., like the flowers, the mountains, the stones and the stars . . .   and if this happens. . .   I'll tell you a wonderful secret: The King of Love himself, whose voice is constantly saying I . . . Love . . . . you . . . to everything, will come from inside, to reign as the King of this Earth . . .   then, you, and me, and everyone will be happy forever and evermore.

Things to Remember

So, if you want a happy planet, where all the people, animals, trees, flowers, stones, mountains and stars feel at the same time The Breath of Love, who sings I . . . . Love . . . . , remember that there are few good things you can do to help.

These are easy, and good, and fun to do.

1.   Feel The Breath of Love everyday.

2.   See everyone as parts of The Breath of Love.

3.   Tell everyone about the Love you feel.

The best way to make a happy planet real is to serve The Breath of Love. To serve IT, makes the heart happy and gives peace and joy, so it is good and fun *to know* and always remember *what* a star, a mountain, a tree, a flower, a rabbit, the teachers, friends, parents, pets, and everyone *really are.*

It's nice to see everything and everyone as parts of The Breath of Love. It's also nice *to know* that you can feel IT right now

If . . . you open your heart and be still . . . Then, you will have It saying to you and the whole Universe: I . . . . Love . . . . I . . . Love . . . . . I . . . . Love . . . .

I must say good-bye now by saying to you with one breath, I Love you - because, although we don't know each other as we *seem to be*, we already know each other as we *really are*. So, we are friends. We are One with The Breath of Love, who pulls all of us together in One Breath, saying always. . . forever. . . I . . . . Love . . . .

So, my dear friend in Love, close your eyes, open your heart and remember . . . Love is always with you! Love is right now breathing you. . . .

Ysatis De Saint Simon

Born in a transatlantic when her parents traveled from Europe to America, Ysatis was exposed since early childhood to people who enriched her spirit and her culture bank of knowledge. After a *'near death experience'* which changed her life almost thirty years ago, she broke her contract as an actress with Universal Studios and became centered in studies of the mind, and through art and philosophy in the evolution of the soul throughout history. Shortly after, she was initiated into the Highest Mystery of Life.

She has written a book about this *Experience*, as her uncle Antoine De Saint-Exupery did himself when he found it and wrote about it in *'The Little Prince'* a book that has been a best seller for years to which she has written a sequel called *'The Return of The Little Prince.'* It is this *Experience* which helped her to understand the sense of being and the essence of her Catholic religion as Jesus taught it and gave her the true dimension of Jesus as the Christ.

Ysatis attributes her youthful and healthy aspect to the faithful practice of this *Experience* and of *'Inner Kung-Fu'* which she later learned from a Chinese master. Her books are thus designed to help others discover their own potential for enlightenment.

For thirty years she has studied in depth the mysteries of early Christianity and other religions, to find the Truth and essential purity which links them all, traveling extensively to different countries where she researched the mysteries of the *'Apocalypse'*, of the lost and original version of *'Genesis'* (as Moses wrote it)*, the mysteries of *The Holy Grail Hallows, the Cup, the Spear and the Holy Shroud of Turin* and has synthesized all of this knowledge into the practice of the *'Science of Being'* as taught by Jesus the Christ and the Great Spiritual Masters of the Ages. In one fashion or another, all of her books and lectures are a reflection of this approach to life.

Ysatis feels that her life is beautiful for she has been successful in finding the Hidden Mystery which gives sense to All, and in helping others to open up to their full potential so that they can also start treading the path towards their own illumination.

Printed in the United States
By Bookmasters